MW00613957

I'M A LITTLE DINGHY ON THE SEA OF LIFE

Little Ira

Fulton Books
Meadville, PA

Published by Fulton Books 2024

The names of the medical professionals have
been altered to protect the author's identity.

ISBN 978-1-63860-342-9 (hardcover)
ISBN 978-1-63860-195-1 (digital)

Printed in the United States of America

CONTENTS

Disclaimer ii
Thank You vii
Meet the Family ix

Part I – I'm a Little Dinghy…

Chapter 1 – Me, Me, Me 1

Prenatal 1
I Am Born 1
Bloodlines 2
Nicknames 3
Problematic Name 4
Biggest Disappointment 6
Second Biggest Disappointment 7
Flatulence 8
Sex 11
I Was Naïve 11
Genitalia Comparisons 12
Fellatio 12
Ego Boost 13

Chapter 2 – The Family 15

The Cow and the Pup 15

The Amusement Park 16
My First Embarrassing Moment 21
Gato! 23
Least Favorite 26
Stepsisters 29
Goosey Lucy..30
Names I Called My Deliverer 31

Chapter 3 – Coworkers...............................33

Smiley 33
The Proposition 34
First Government Job 35
Pardon? 37
Open Mouth, Insert Foot......................38
Hairdo...39
Sour Apple 40

Chapter 4 – Doctors 42

Family Physician....................................42
Where's My Bite?....................................45
The "Hyst" Heist.....................................51
One Hemorrhoid 59
Mental Images..61
Breast Augmentation 62

Part II – ...On the Sea of Life

Chapter 1 – Myalgic Encephalomyelitis.................75

Symptoms 84
Fatigue and Stress 84

iv

Ringing in My Ears 85
Inability to Concentrate..................85
Cold Extremities...........................87
Burning Sensations 87
Sharp Pains.................................88
Spatial Impairment........................88
Immunizations 88

Chapter 2 – Suicide Attempt 90

Chapter 3 – Allergies 96

Chapter 4 – Marriage And Divorce..................104

Growing Up 104
My Mother.................................104
My Father.................................105
Courtship.................................106
Marriage..................................108
Meet Mr. Real 109
Living with Mr. Real......................112
The Rope 113
Sleeping Arrangements 114
Guilt Trip Routines.......................116
Sexual Relations..........................116
Orgasms 118
Fantasizing Begins 118
Coworker's Advice 119
Fantasizing Ends..........................120
Hysterectomy 121

Carrot of Hope 122
Not Your Responsibility 122
Bag of Peas 124
Psychologist 124
Personal Torment 127
Infusions 127
Attitude Adjustment 129
Divorce 131
The Rope 131
Happy/Unhappy 132
Dividing Assets 133
Gifts? 134
Survivor Benefits 134
Too Little, Too Late 135
Duty Done 136

Epilogue 139

Introduction 139
Thermostats 139
Do You Smell Gas? 140
Where Did I Put It? 141
Facial Expression 141
Q-Tips 142
The Mounds Bar 143
Man in the Street 144
The Sneeze 146
Pencil Drawings 146

THANK YOU

The first thing I wrote was Part II, Chapter 4. Once completed, I sent copies to my family members.

After my second cousin read his copy, he called. We discussed it in great detail.

During this conversation, he said, "You should write a book."

Thank you, Loren, for planting that seed.

MEET THE FAMILY

"Babe"–Luanne's paternal grandmother
Barbara–paternal half sister
"Ern"–Luanne's paternal grandfather
Daniel–Lucy Diane's husband
David–nephew; Luanne's son
Florence "Flo"–maternal aunt
Henry "Tony"–step-cousin, Taede's eldest child and only son
Jerry–maternal cousin; Florence and Bud's middle child
John "Bud"–maternal uncle by marriage; Florence's husband
Judith "Judi"–maternal cousin; Florence and Bud's younger daughter
Leona "Sis/Sissie"–maternal great-aunt; Mary's youngest sister
Leslie "Les"–father; Lucy's second husband
Luanne–maternal half sister; Lucy's older daughter
Lucy "Lou"–mother
Mary "Mame"–maternal grandmother
Phyllis "Phyl"–maternal cousin; Florence and Bud's eldest daughter
Richard "Dick"–maternal great-uncle; Roy's youngest brother

Raymond "Ray"–maternal cousin; Roma's son with first husband

Roma "Ro"–maternal aunt

Roy–maternal grandfather

Sandra "San"–maternal cousin; Roma and Ted's older daughter

Sarah Margaret "Maggie"–maternal great-grandmother; Leona and Mary's mother

Sharon–maternal cousin; Roma and Ted's younger daughter

Taede "Ted"/"Dutch"–maternal uncle by marriage; Roma's second husband

Theresa "Tress"–step-cousin; Taede's eldest daughter

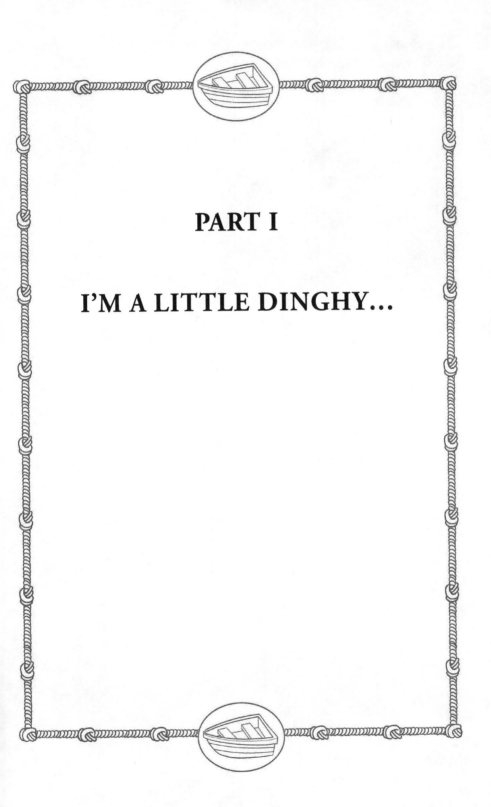

PART I

I'M A LITTLE DINGHY...

CHAPTER 1

ME, ME, ME

Prenatal

My father, Leslie, had been widowed twice and divorced once. His second marriage produced a daughter, Barbara. My mother, Lucy, had been widowed when she was pregnant with her daughter, Luanne.

My maternal grandfather, Roy, had been blessed with four granddaughters and two grandsons.

When Mom became pregnant with me, Grampa Roy and my father thought a boy was an excellent idea. To tip the balance in their direction, Grampa began referring to me as Little Ira.

I Am Born

It was a spring day in a southern California town. World War II was raging in Europe and the Pacific. When I arrived at the hospital, I weighed in at eight pounds, five and a half ounces.

During Mom's ten-day stay, she became friendly with the woman who cleaned the floors. One morning, I was with Mom when she entered the room.

"Oh," she said, "What a pretty baby! What did you name her?"

"Lucy Diane."

"Was it after an old maiden aunt?"

"No," Mom replied. "I named her after myself."

Since Mom was called Lucy, I was dubbed Diane.

Bloodlines

Between my father and mother, I received a variety of bloodlines. I think I have the traits that are considered characteristic of each culture I represent.

English: Far too often the punch line of a joke has to be explained to me because I just don't "get" it.

Scottish: Frugality is my second middle name.

Irish: When there is a twinkle in my eye, 'tis herself is present and a mischievous leprechaun is perched upon my right shoulder.

Greek: I didn't get enough of this blood to resemble a goddess, but I did get enough for the black mustache.

Cherokee: According to Gramma Maggie, I have a few drops of this blood which gave me my high cheekbones, and without trying, I can walk up behind someone unheard.

Scotch-Irish: I have always assumed that the traits of my pure Scottish and Irish bloodlines were simply enhanced by a combination of the two.

I think the story of how the Scotch-Irish connection began is interesting. History tells that there were a few clans in Scotland that England could not subdue. The British finally proposed to these clans that they would be given lands and titles in Ireland, *if* they swore they would stop their rebellious behavior. The clans, of course, jumped at the chance. The Scotsmen were delighted with their good fortune; the Irish inhabitants were not.

When my sister, Barbara, traveled to Ireland, she found that the Irish people still resent Britain's deal with the Scottish clans.

Nicknames

When we were children, Luanne and I had four female cousins living in the vicinity. We spent so much time together it was as though we were all sisters. Each of us had a nickname—mine was "Bugs." I never knew if I got that name because of my aversion to the insect kingdom or because I had large protruding front teeth that made me resemble Bugs Bunny.

My immediate family, and sometimes the extended family, called me Dizee (DIE-zee). Mom's older sister, Roma, called me Digee (DIE-gee).

Aunt Florence, Mom's younger sister, called me "Anths," and I do know when I received that nickname. She stopped by one afternoon to visit with Mom. I was outside playing in the yard, unaware that I had chosen to sit next to an ant hill. At that time, I spoke with a lisp. When I discovered the ants crawling on me, I ran into the house yelling, "Mama! Mama! Anths! Anths! Get them off me!"

Later in life, I had one coworker who called me Deeann (DEE-ann) and a close friend of my husband who called me Diannie (DIE-annie).

Problematic Name

When I entered grade school, the lifelong problem with my name began. Because I was named Lucy Diane, everyone assumed I would be called Lucy.

With each new teacher in grade school and the numerous instructors I encountered in high school, I had to explain to each and every one why I was called Diane.

After graduation, the problem continued to rear its ugly head every time I gave my name for the first time to someone new, i.e., employers, doctors, dentists, orthodontist, periodontist, hospital staff, insurance companies and bankers.

When I had been in the workplace for six years, I decided to apply for a job with the federal government. 'This time,' I thought, 'I'll try something different with my name.'

In the space on the form which requested my first name, I entered "L. (i. o.)." The "i. o." acronym means "initial only." In the space marked for middle initial, I entered, "Diane."

It worked like a charm. I didn't have to make any explanations.

There were two places that refused to accept a name that did not exactly match the name on my birth certificate— the driver's license bureau and the insurance company.

Using L. Diane as my name worked beautifully for forty years. In the first decade of the twenty-first century, when I turned sixty-five, a change occurred.

I called the Social Security Administration's toll free number to make arrangements to set up a payment plan for my Medicare benefits.

The nice gentleman I spoke with had easy access to my SSN (Social Security Number) that listed my name as it appears on my birth certificate. I explained to him the difficulties I had had my entire life by being called by my middle name.

I also explained that I had gone by L. Diane most of my adult life, and that was the name that appeared on ninety-nine percent of my legal documents.

I asked, "May I use L. Diane for Medicare purposes?"

"No."

"How about Diane?"

"No."

"L. D.?"

"No."

The name on my Medicare card reads, "Lucy D."

This change required me to write numerous letters to physicians, laboratories, pharmacies, the hospital and health insurance companies notifying them that my name would now appear as Lucy D. rather than L. Diane.

I now have two identities.

When I call to schedule a doctor's appointment, request a prescription, or go into a facility that accepts Medicare, I have to remember "who I am." In the medical world, I am Lucy D.; to everyone else, I am Diane.

Once again, my name has become problematic.

Biggest Disappointment

During my childhood I had overheard tidbits about sex by the adult women in my extended family. When I became an adolescent, the sexual connotations in magazine ads, movies and on television were impossible to ignore. In high school, I sometimes overheard whispered sex-related conversations in the girls' locker room.

I was convinced that the act of sexual intercourse would produce an indescribable ecstasy that would be heralded by bells, whistles and fireworks.

When I was sixteen, I was allowed to wear earrings and lipstick and go on dates with boys. I enjoyed the romance, and of course, the kissing. As is normal, I was becoming sexually aroused by these activities.

As was dictated for girls of my generation, I was supposed to remain a virgin until I married. I waited until I was eighteen years old and a senior in high school. It was baccalaureate night which took place at the high school gym. After the ceremony, I went out with my current beau.

I was wearing a shocking pink, snug-fitting wool dress that was fully lined. The long-sleeved matching jacket fit tightly at the waist when buttoned and had a shawl collar. I wore white accessories, which included a pearl necklace and earrings, gloves, purse and a pair of three-inch spike-heeled shoes with pointed toes.

Since the ceremony had taken place on Sunday night, my curfew was early. My beau and I drove out to one of the many deserted country roads in our area and parked.

In the back seat of his car, we began petting. One thing led to another, and we had intercourse (in my day it was called doing "it"). We were in the missionary position when I was penetrated for the first time. He did the required in and out strokes. No bells. I waited. No whistles. I waited. No fireworks. I waited. A few minutes later, he had an orgasm. It was over.

My only thought was, '*This* is "it"? *This* is what all the shouting is about? I wadded up my new shocking pink wool skirt for *this*! Someone has *got* to be joking!'

<u>Second Biggest Disappointment</u>

It was October in the late seventies when my husband, Daniel, and I flew to Boston with a travel club we had joined the previous year. He had been stationed at Fort Devon when he was in the Army and was familiar with the area. It was my first trip to New England.

On the second day of our vacation, we headed to the Plymouth Plantation. The first stop was at the replica of the Mayflower. The tour was interesting. Seeing each section of the ship made me extremely grateful that I would never have to travel in such cramped quarters.

Next, we came to the replicas of the pilgrims' tiny abodes. Each had its own small garden plot, and there were people dressed in period costumes, going about their daily chores.

What I had come to see was Plymouth Rock. Not far past the houses, there was a sign directing us down a path. As we followed the signs, I kept looking in all directions trying to see it. The last sign indicated that we should climb a few steps and cross an arched cement bridge which covered a small, sandy gully.

When we got to the middle of the bridge, I looked north, I looked south, I looked east and west. I saw nothing.

Daniel said, "Here it is!"

"Where?"

Pointing down, he said, "Here."

With a quizzical look on my face, I walked to where he was standing and looked down. At our feet was a metal grate set in the cement. I bent at the waist and peered through the bars.

Several feet below was a small white rock nestled in the sand. When I squinted my eyes, I was able to make out the "1640" carved into the stone.

Considering I had been expecting a scaled-down version of the Rock of Gibraltar, I was sorely disappointed.

Flatulence

The women in my Mom's family were prone to flatulence.

When I was in my early teens, I recall going to my Great-Aunt Leona's house for lunch. The guests included

Great-Gramma Maggie, who lived with Leona, Gramma Mary, Mom, Aunt Florence, my sister Luanne, and me.

You should know that Luanne disapproved of flatulence. She considered it disgusting behavior and thought it should occur, only if it could not be avoided, in the confines of the bathroom.

Everyone else attending the party considered flatulence as a form of entertainment.

After imbibing a delicious lunch, everyone went into Leona's spacious living room and sat down to visit.

It wasn't long before an audible flatulence noise was heard.

Someone asked, "Is that the best you can do?"

"Think you can beat it?" was the response.

"Of course, I can!" An even louder blast filled the room. The giggles began and the contest was on.

My young digestive system kept me from participating.

The contestants performed at will. Unfortunately, I do not remember who was declared the winner.

Gramma Maggie enjoyed the contest more than anyone else. Her laughter shook her tiny frame as tears of joy rolled down her cheeks.

She was a frail woman who was no longer able to get out and about. Because of that, she took advantage of social gatherings to wear her jewelry. There were numerous necklaces hanging at various lengths from her neck and several bracelets going up each arm.

She wore a pair of sizable diamond stud earrings which were never removed. Those earrings had been purchased as a gift to herself when she retired from a confectioner's company in Kansas City.

My fondest memory of that day is a room filled with the women I loved and their laughter.

*****

I was seldom around my father's family so I do not know if he had any gaseous relatives. Dad rarely passed gas. When he did, it was a barely audible, "pfft." He was no contest contender.

With age, I began producing larger amounts of gas. Considering Mom's **kaboom** and Dad's "pfft," it's logical that my gaseous releases fell into the medium range.

*****

My husband, Daniel, and I had vastly different sleeping habits. He fell asleep two minutes after his head hit the pillow. I felt fortunate if I dozed off after an hour.

One night, we had been in bed for fifteen minutes. Daniel was sound asleep.

I began passing motorboat flatulence. You know the kind—putt, putt, putt, putt, putt, putt.

Halfway through, Daniel began to rouse. He rolled over and began reaching for the clock radio.

"What are you doing?" I asked.

"It's time to get up. I'm trying to turn off the alarm."

"It's *not* the alarm. I'm passing gas! Go back to sleep."

*****

The odor of my flatulence is dependent upon the foods I eat. One night, after eating a delicious dinner that my digestive tract did not like, Daniel and I went to bed at the usual time.

We were both lying on our left sides. As soon as I got comfy, I passed some gas.

A few seconds later, Daniel threw off his covers, ran to the window and opened it as wide as it would go.

I turned over.

His nose was pressed against the screen, and he was sucking in vast amounts of cool evening air.

"What are you doing?" I asked.

"Jesus Christ! That one made my eyes water!"

Sex

I Was Naïve

The females of my immediate and extended family sheltered me from harm and from information deemed inappropriate.

My Gramma Mary would never say pregnant aloud. She would lean close to another adult female family member, put her hand against the side of her mouth and whisper, "I heard she's PG."

Since that information was hush-hush, it's easy to understand why my sexual education was lacking.

Until I was twenty years old, if someone had said "oral sex" to me, I would have thought they wanted to discuss the subject.

Genitalia Comparisons

The male penis is a versatile appendage. Depending on the male's mindset, his penis will either be looking at the floor or proudly pointing at the ceiling.

The male can use his penis to write his name in the snow and compete with other males to see who can urinate farthest.

On the other hand, the female genitalia is like Brand X cereal. It simply lies there and gets soggy.

Fellatio

I was in my twenties before I became knowledgeable about sexual practices that differed from having intercourse in the missionary position.

Eventually, I became acquainted with orally stimulating the penis. However, the thought of performing fellatio made me extremely uncomfortable. After years of performing oral stimulation, I began trying to psych myself up to the point that I could perform fellatio.

The thought of bodily excretions was disconcerting. To me, fecal matter and urine turned my stomach. Even sweat was unpleasant to my way of thinking. I had heard that some women thought sweaty men were sensuous. Personally, I don't want an odorous man anywhere near me. I much prefer a man who has just stepped out of the shower, dried off, and has secured the towel snugly around his waist.

The only bodily excretion I found acceptable were tears. I finally convinced myself that if I thought only about tears during the act of fellatio, I would be all right.

Eventually, I tried out my theory. When the orgasm occurred, it was not what I had anticipated. First I choked; then I gagged. I made a beeline for the bathroom and hung my head over the toilet bowl because I thought I was going to throw up.

It was then that I realized I could not equate an orgasm with tears because tears don't squirt.

<u>Ego Boost</u>

Shortly before reaching retirement age, I became hypersensitive to chemical odors. Because of the problem, I began wearing a painter's mask in certain places to alleviate the irritation. Stores selling paints, fertilizers, mothballs, scented candles and perfumes required that accessory.

When I was preparing to move out of the Denver area, I went shopping at a Bed, Bath and Beyond establishment. As soon as I walked through the door, I donned the mask.

I began browsing and selecting various items I would need after the move. Some of the store's aisles provided just enough space for two buggies to pass one another as long as one's fingers were kept to the middle of the push bar.

As I was walking down one of these aisles, a young man and his son, who was seated inside the buggy, approached me.

When the boy saw me, his eyes grew large, and his mouth fell open. He kept a close eye on me as our buggies passed within inches of one another.

After passing, I heard him say, "Dad, why is that lady wearing a mask?"

His father responded, "Because she's Super Woman!"

Even though it was hidden by the mask, there was a big smile on my face. I said over my left shoulder, "Thank you!"

Over his left shoulder, he replied, "You're welcome."

CHAPTER 2

THE FAMILY

The Cow and the Pup

Uncle Ted was the only rich person I have ever known. He and his first wife, Boukja, who was in poor health, and their infant son, Tony, immigrated to America from Holland through Ellis Island. Tony's given name was Henry Jan, but from the time he was born, his mother called him Tony, which in Dutch, means fat boy. He may have been fat as a boy, but he grew into a very tall, lanky man.

Uncle Ted bought land in one of southern California's valleys and began a dairy farm. Boukja gave birth to a baby girl, Theresa, and later succumbed to her illness. She died from tuberculosis.

When that happened, Uncle Ted needed someone to care for his home and his young children. He hired my Aunt Roma, who had a young son, Raymond.

Roma and Ted liked one another and got along so well that, for convenience, they married. Their union produced two daughters, Sandra and Sharon, and Uncle Ted "adopted" Roma's extended family as his own.

After Grampa Roy and Gramma Mary separated, Gramma would travel to California for visits. Sometimes, she prolonged her stay. Uncle Ted was very fond of Gramma and liked having her living at the ranch. He also enjoyed teasing her.

Gramma was a tall, thin, wiry woman with deep-set dark eyes and black hair. I inherited my high cheekbones from her.

Ted had a scrawny, sway-backed milk cow. He told Mary that he had decided to call the cow, "Mame," which was Gramma's nickname.

Gramma was not phased. She bided her time.

Not long after the cow-naming incident, Gramma got a puppy. She named him "Teddy."

I don't know how long "Mame" lived, but "Teddy" lived to be a toothless, almost hairless, elderly gentleman who was beloved by everyone in the family.

The Amusement Park

My first experience at the Lakeside Amusement Park, located in north Denver, occurred in the early fifties. It was the summer prior to my family's move from California to Colorado.

Mom and several members of her family worked at the park. Grampa Roy operated rides. Gramma Mary, Great-Aunt Leona, Aunt Roma and Mom sold tickets to the rides. Cousins Phyllis and Jerry worked there, too. Phyllis worked in the office and the food court. Jerry worked at the swimming pool and carried change to the ticket sellers and returned cash to the office.

The park had two entrances. One was at the south end of the park where Kiddie Land was located. The other entry point was the main gate on Sheridan Boulevard. I liked the main entrance because as you walked through its archway, there was a magnificent view of the lake—which was named after the owner's daughter, Rhoda—and the colored lights on the rides. Even in the midday sun, the lights were noticeable. After dark, they were dazzling. I then got to walk down the wide wooden staircase that led into the park.

At the bottom of the staircase and to the right was a food court. The hamburgers they sold were the thinnest I have ever seen. All it took to cook one well done was to slap it onto the grill, smash it with a spatula, flip it over, smash it again and place it on the bun. To my taste buds, they were always delicious.

To the left of the staircase were concession stands and the arcades. We sometimes stopped for a snow cone or cotton candy. The paper cup holding the flavored ice was never sturdy enough for me. The few times I got one—always red—it invariable ended up on my dress or the cement.

Pink cotton candy was a more stable treat. The first time I had one, I began eating it by taking little bites. Having my nose and hair covered with sticky spun sugar was not ideal. After that, I began pulling globs of the cotton candy off and stuffing it into my mouth, which was a far better technique.

On our occasional trips to the park when the family was working, Luanne and I along with our cousins, Judi, Sandra and Sharon, were each allowed one free ride where a family member worked.

I remember a ride on the Whip when Mom was selling tickets and one on the Rocket Ships where Aunt Roma was working that day.

Grampa Roy allowed me one ride per visit on the Tilt-a-Whirl, the Tumblebug, the Frolic or the Star Ride. He frequently operated one of my favorite rides—the Merry-Go-Round.

Another favorite was the trains that traveled around Lake Rhoda. One was rustic and had wooden seats. I preferred the other one because the passengers were more enclosed and the seats were cushioned. In my mind, I was riding on the Union Pacific's Zephyr.

On one of the visits to the park, I was thrilled when I heard Grampa was operating the trains. When I asked him for my ride, he said, "No, this one costs too much."

His answer surprised me. I didn't know that the family paid for our free rides.

I learned a valuable lesson that day. Not only did I come from a loving family, I also came from a family with integrity.

The most expensive ride in the park was the Speed Boats. It took passengers around the lake which I never experienced. It was, however, free to walk onto their dock and admire the boat's sleek, well-polished mahogany exterior and its leather seats.

The lake water around the dock was teeming with fish that my family called "suckers." They were corn-fed and *fat*. People would walk onto the dock, drop pieces of popcorn into the water, and then watch the feeding frenzy caused by the fish trying to get their fair share. I was mesmerized by the sight of those gray fish with their large, gaping mouths sucking in each treasured piece of popcorn. If you stood too close to the rail, you'd get wet from their frantic splashing.

The Fun House *sounded* like it would be fun. When I entered, I realized it wasn't. There were holes drilled into the wooden floor where a shot of compressed air could be expelled. When timed correctly, that air made girls' skirts fly above their heads. I was an extremely modest child and that exposure embarrassed me. I did venture down one of the very high slides once. On the way down, my skirt slipped out from under my legs, and my bare flesh skidded on the slide's metal surface which left a red abrasion.

The only thing I did like about the Fun House was on its outside. Atop the building was an enormous mechanical fat lady mannequin. She would lean forward and then back while her loud, cackling laughter resounded throughout the park. Her laughter always made me smile.

The most memorable Fourth of July of my life was spent at the park. I was seated on the grass next to the lake near the Rocket Ship ride for their spectacular fireworks display. One of the fireworks shot high into the night sky, and when it burst, thousands of large shiny white stars rained down into the water. When they touched the surface, there was a hissing sound and steam rose from the water. That scene, which is still vivid in my mind's eye, was the most beautiful thing I have ever seen.

*****

Grampa Roy worked at the amusement park long after everyone else in the family. When each summer season ended, he hooked his small, one-bedroom trailer to his light blue, two-door coupe, with its metal sun visor attached above the windshield, and headed south.

He wintered in Arizona with the other snowbirds and enjoyed the sunshine and warmth that state provided. Each spring, he returned to Colorado. He situated his "home" in a trailer park nearby and worked for another season.

Although I do not recall the circumstances, one year, in midsummer, Grampa Roy parked his trailer in our side yard for a couple of weeks.

Grampa didn't have much, so his home was always neat and clean. After dark, being inside was especially pleasant. Because of his low-wattage bulbs, there was a warm glow that emanated from his highly polished alder cabinet doors. I was fascinated by the way the doors were opened. To get inside each one, you pressed two cream-colored plastic squares toward the center of the latch.

Grampa's trailer had a scent all its own. It was a combination of the summer's heat, furniture polish, and the sweet aroma coming from the cherry blend tobacco he smoked in his pipe.

My First Embarrassing Moment

Luanne's paternal grandparents, Babe and Ern, lived in a small town near the eastern slope of the Colorado mountains. They had an older, two-story house with a porch that ran the full length of its front. There were wide steps, without railings, in the middle of the porch that led to its painted wooden floor, and it had a roof to ward off the elements. To me, it was beautiful.

In my young mind, it seemed as though they had a gigantic yard which had the greenest grass and the most beautiful flowers I had ever seen.

On the west side of the property was an irrigation ditch. Just above the water line, there was grass with its long blades dipping into the slow moving water that was headed south. Above the grass were clumps of various varieties of colorful flowers. Between the two, the dirt was weed-free. There was a well-kept narrow wooden bridge that carried a person across the water.

On the other side was a triangular piece of fenced ground which enclosed a large shade tree, a small shelter and a brown horse with a white patch on his face. I loved it when he would amble to my side of the fence and let me pet his soft, velvety nose.

Behind the house were a few outbuildings. Gramma and Grampa had chickens and geese. The chickens were fenced; the geese roamed freely. The geese did not take kindly to trespassers in their yard. Anytime they spied me walking around, they headed toward me with their necks outstretched, their clipped wings flapping and their beaks set to go nip, nip, nip. Their attack squawks were unmistakable. When I heard that sound, I knew danger was approaching, and I made a mad dash to the steep back steps that led to the safety of Gramma's kitchen.

When entering their house through the front door, you stepped into a spacious living room. To the west was a large dining room. Behind the dining room was a farm-house-style kitchen. Entry to their master bedroom was through French doors off the living room. The staircase to the second floor bedrooms lay between the kitchen and master bedroom. The one drawback to this gracious home was that its only bathroom was located on the second floor.

In the northeast corner of the living room was Gramma and Grampa's player piano with many rolls of music neatly stacked in their boxes atop this magical instrument.

My sister, Luanne, and I were allowed to play one roll each. We selected the music that we knew the words to so that we, and Mama, could sing along. I loved pumping the pedals, and with my hands in my lap, watching the keys depressing themselves as the music played.

Gramma was an excellent cook and her meals were always sumptuous and delicious. An hour after one of those meals, I walked from the kitchen, through the dining room, and as I entered the living room, Grampa walked up to me.

He held out his right index finger. "Would you pull this for me?"

Dutifully, I did as he asked. As I pulled, he flatulated—loudly!

He laughed; I did not. I froze in my tracks. I could feel my face heating up and knew it was turning bright red.

To this day, I cannot remember what happened next.

Gato!

Grampa Roy was a printer by profession. His father had owned and operated a weekly paper in the same town where Babe and Ern lived. Grampa Roy had operated a weekly paper in the town where I grew up.

Later in life, he was hired by the railroad to operate the town's depot. During his tenure, freight trains were the only thing traveling the tracks. They ran north and south through the middle of our community.

When I walked through the door of the depot into his office, I was greeted with the smell of the well-oiled old wooden floor. To the right of the door was a tall workbench. It had a bookshelf atop it, and the shelves had many narrow cubby holes where Grampa sorted his paperwork. On the left sat a rolltop desk and a rocking, swiveling, rolling wooden office chair with arms. Whenever Grampa rocked, swiveled or rolled, the chair's mechanisms squeaked loudly.

Halfway across the room, on the bench side, was a small, round coal stove with ornate chrome bands—one at the top; the other nearer the bottom. The door in its midsection opened so that coal or wood could be added. A round section on the stove's top could be lifted using a specific tool designed for that purpose. I never knew why it was removable. When the flat top was in place, Grampa could heat a pot of coffee or his supper.

To the right of the stove was a straight-backed wooden dining room chair. On the left was a wooden captain's chair. I loved that chair's barrel-shaped design even though it was uncomfortable. I didn't let a little discomfort deter me because that's where I always seated myself.

On the floor behind the stove sat two open case boxes of canned food. One box contained Dinty-Moore stew; the other, peaches.

Through a door on the west side of the office was another room where Grampa had his bed and a wardrobe.

Our house was located several blocks from the depot, and it had a very small kitchen. The east wall had the sink and cupboards. There was just enough space on the west wall for the refrigerator and a narrow metal cabinet. The gas stove was on the south.

The red-and-chrome kitchen table and four chairs fit tightly against the north wall. Two people could pass one another when the chairs were under the table. When they were out, only one person could get through.

When my father was at the table, he sat at the end next to the cupboards. When he wasn't at home, it was Mom's spot. Whenever someone came to visit on weekdays, they sat at the opposite end of the table from her.

Whenever Mom had a banana that no one would eat and was unfit for baking a cake, she saved it for Grampa Roy. According to him a banana was not ripe until it was totally black. He would place the banana on a plate, cut the skin with a sharp knife, and scooped out the mushy, golden-colored fruit with a spoon.

Many years later, I saw one of the well-known television cooks talking about bananas. According to her, a banana was ripe when "freckles" appeared on the skin. At that stage the fruit was perfect for eating, cooking or baking. She firmly stated that a black banana should never be used because it had fermented.

That information put a big smile on my face. Grampa Roy had always been a teetotaler—except for his bananas!

Another thing he enjoyed doing was teasing our big black-and-white cat Mama had named Ignatz—Iggy to the family. I didn't like it when Grampa upset him.

One afternoon, he was sitting at the kitchen table visiting with Mom. Iggy and I came into the kitchen from the living room with Iggy leading the way.

As soon as Grampa saw him, he did his "usual thing." He rapidly stamped his feet up and down on the linoleum covered floor and began making a weird high-pitched sound. His finale was saying loudly, "*Gato!*"

Iggy's reaction to Grampa's teasing was always the same. His body tensed as he froze in his tracks. His back arched, his hair stood on end, and he bared his teeth as he hissed.

On that particular day, I had had enough. I planted my ten-year-old body directly in front of him. Standing akimbo and using the most severe voice I could muster, I said, "Grampa! That's *not* nice, and you *shouldn't* do it!"

The look on Grampa's face was utter disbelief. Here was his shy, timid, always-hiding-behind-her-mother's-skirt granddaughter standing up to him.

A few seconds later, a tiny grin began to appear on his lips. His blue eyes began to twinkle, and he threw his head back and howled with laughter.

Did my ten-year-old admonishment of Grampa Roy alter his behavior? Not one bit.

Least Favorite

My Great-Gramma, Maggie, was a small woman with a deeply wrinkled face and sparkling blue eyes.

No matter where Gramma lived, she took her porch swing and attached it to her new porch roof, and she always found the perfect spot to plant her moss roses. I was fascinated by those plants because they produced blossoms of various colors on the same stem. I especially liked the years when Gramma planted them in a discarded tractor tire filled with dirt.

She had a black cocker spaniel named Gypsy. When it was time for Gypsy to come home, Gramma would stand on the porch and shout, "**GYPSY!!!**"

It was hard to believe that that voice had come from such a tiny person. I don't know how Gypsy responded, but I would have "come a running!"

*****

I was a child who always wanted to be helpful. When I went to Gramma Maggie's house one afternoon, she was in her kitchen peeling carrots.

"Can I do something to help, Gramma?" I asked.

"Yes," she said as she handed me two carrots. "Take them on the porch and let the peelings drop on the dirt."

I took the carrots. She handed me a paring knife. I didn't take it.

"Don't you have a vegetable peeler, Gramma?"

"No," she said angrily, "I do not. Just take the knife and do the best you can!"

I did as she said. As I was heading for the back door, I heard her mumbling under her breath. "Kids today can't do *anything* unless they have some newfangled gadget!"

I used the paring knife and tried very hard to accomplish the task. When I handed the carrots back to Gramma, they were half their original thickness.

*****

There was a period of time when the extended family got together on Friday nights and played the board game, Royal Rummy. It always took place at Gramma Mary's house. My sister and cousins entertained themselves elsewhere; I sat quietly and watched the adults play.

Sometimes when Uncle Bud or Cousin Jerry needed to use the outhouse, they allowed me to play their hand. I took my responsibility seriously. Playing cards with the grown-ups made me feel important.

When each hand was completed, the players put a penny on their designated space on the board. Gramma Maggie always seated herself by the King and Queen of Hearts or its next-door neighbor, the 6, 7, 8 of any suit. It was rare for anyone to win either of them, so Gramma

Mary placed a clear custard dish at each one to hold the pennies as they accumulated. By evening's end, the dishes were filled to their brims.

Gramma Maggie kept her pennies, and occasionally a nickel and a dime, in a one-quart plastic measuring cup she held on her lap as she played. When the cards were being dealt for the next hand by someone else, she would run her fingers through the coins.

When she was winning, there were many coins, and she smiled broadly as she rearranged the money in her cup. When she had a losing night, her expression was serious as she picked up each coin in its turn, rubbed it between her thumb and middle finger, and returned it to the bottom of the cup.

I was sitting next to her on one of the evenings when she was losing. There were only a few pennies left. When a hand ended, the cards were picked up and given to the next dealer. As everyone was placing their penny on the board to ante up for the next hand, I noticed that Gramma Maggie didn't put a coin in the almost full custard cup in front of her.

I said, "Gramma, you haven't put your penny in the cup yet."

She leaned toward me; I leaned toward her.

Out of the side of her mouth, she hissed under her breath, "Shut up!"

Stepsisters

Some people have a problem trying to figure out my family. To me, it is quite simple. My father was married and had a daughter. Mom was married and had a daughter. They married and had me. Ergo, I have two half sisters, and they each have one half sister and one stepsister.

When my parents married, my father's daughter, Barbara, was eleven, and Mom's daughter, Luanne, was three.

Having been an only child for so many years, Barbara did not like sharing attention with Luanne. At every opportunity, when Mom wasn't around, Barbara was hateful to her young stepsister. She continued this behavior into our adult lives.

When I was eight years old, Mom, Dad, Luanne and I moved to Colorado. Barbara was married and had a two-year-old daughter. She and her family remained in California.

Eight years later, Barbara *honored* us with one of her visits. On this trip, she had traveled alone and was staying at the house with Mom, Dad and me.

Luanne was now married, and one evening during Barbara's visit, she and her husband, Roy, came to the house for dinner. Afterward, everyone moved to the living room to visit.

Around eight o'clock Barbara said she was going to remove her make-up and get ready for bed.

When she returned to the living room, Luanne let out a bloodcurdling scream that sounded as if someone had just cut off her hand with a hatchet!

Every eye was on Luanne. We were so shocked, we were speechless.

Looking directly at Barbara, Luanne said in a quiet, calm voice, "Oh, I'm sorry. I didn't recognize you without your make-up."

Revenge *is* sweet!

Goosey Lucy

Mom always said she was "goosey" which I thought meant that she didn't like having her buttocks touched. Since I had never touched her in that location, I was none the wiser.

When Mom was in her late sixties, she moved into an eighteen-story high-rise apartment building for seniors. She was on the seventeenth floor, and her apartment faced west.

Her view of the Rocky Mountains was spectacular. When the Lakeside Amusement Park had their Fourth of July fireworks, Mom sat by her window, looked to the northwest, and enjoyed their colorful display.

When Daniel and I took Mom out, we went in our sedan. Mom rode in the front passenger seat because it was easier for her to get her left leg prosthesis into the car.

One Thanksgiving, there was a heavy snowstorm. Daniel cleared a portion of our driveway so we could get one vehicle out to the street. He put chains on the wheels of our pickup truck and off we went.

Mama was waiting for us in the lobby of her building. She was bundled up in a heavy winter coat, gloves, faux fur hat and boots.

We parked on the east side of the building as their parking lot on the west, where we usually picked her up, had not been cleared. Daniel parked as close to the curb as he could. Mom met us at the door, and we walked on either side of her to the truck. Daniel opened the passenger side door.

This was a new experience for Mom as she had not gotten into a truck since her leg amputation. She began the attempt, but only managed to get partially into the cab.

Daniel headed to the driver's side door thinking he might be able to pull her in.

When he left, I stood behind Mom. I thought, 'If I give her a gentle boost on her bottom, perhaps that would help.' She was so well-padded I didn't think it would cause a problem.

I placed both hands on her back side and gently gave her a boost.

Mom shot across the cab to the driver's side door like a roman candle!

I now knew the exact meaning of a being "goosey."

Names I Called My Deliverer

The last five years of Mom's life were spent in a nursing home. Once she had adjusted to her surroundings, we set up a day and time each week when I called her. During one of these visits, she asked, "What names have you called me?"

"Mostly, I've called you Mom, Mama or Ma. Of course, later in life, I started calling you Lou, and on occasion, Lulu. Why do you ask?"

"I can hear you calling me, Mother."

"Mother? I don't think…" I thought for a moment and then recalled something.

"Did it sound like, 'Yeeeeeeees, Mother;' 'Noooooooo, Mother'?"

"That's it! That's *exactly* it!"

I laughed. "Honey, the only time I said that was when you told me something I didn't want to hear."

"Like what?"

"Oh, you'd say, you *should* do this, or, you *shouldn't* do that, and I'd respond with, 'Yeeeeeeeees, Mother;' 'Noooooooo, Mother.'"

CHAPTER 3

COWORKERS

<u>Smiley</u>

My first full-time job was with a government-contracted company located on Colorado's front range. The employees referred to this sprawling facility as the "Plant."

I was eighteen years old and had just graduated from high school. I took typing classes in my junior and senior years, and my teacher told me, "You will never make a living as a typist."

When I took the typing test at the Plant, I failed. The fact that my father was an employee might explain why I was hired. My assigned position was in the office that kept track of secret documents located at the facility. My duties required only a minimal amount of typing.

One of my functions was signing for classified documents which were delivered twice daily by one of the Plant's armed guards. The majority of these men were very pleasant. There was, however, one man who was the grumpiest person I had ever met. It seemed to me that he delivered documents more frequently than the other guards, and I was certain that the scowl on his face was permanent.

For months, whenever he came into the office, I would smile and convey a pleasant greeting; he maintained his scowl and would mumble something unintelligible under his breath.

One morning, I was feeling especially cheerful. When he came in, I gave him my biggest smile and said, "Good morning, Smiley!"

He burst into uproarious laughter which left me and my coworkers with our mouths hanging open.

I don't know how he greeted other employees after that, but he always gave me a big smile and a cheerful, "Hello!"

The Proposition

While working at my first job, I learned how to operate an electric typewriter. Its quick response to my fingers' touch was startling, but eventually, I adjusted to its rapidity. With practice, I finally managed to pass the company's typing test.

I applied for a secretarial position and was selected by a supervisor in the same building. Ed was a tall, well-built man in his forties with salt-and-pepper hair. The secretary with the most seniority in our department called him "Rosebud" because of his beautifully shaped lips.

I was a naive twenty-year-old with no self-confidence and was terrified I would lose my position if I made too many mistakes.

One morning, I was working in the top drawer of a file cabinet and was facing the wall. Ed came up behind me.

Our bodies were not touching, but I could feel his warm breath on the back of my neck.

In his quiet voice he said, "I have a proposition for you."

My body tensed and my eyes grew to the size of saucers. I was grateful that he could not see my face.

I said nothing.

He continued, "If you'll go and get me a cup of coffee, I'll buy you one."

My body relaxed, and my eyes returned to normal. I turned around wearing my usual broad smile. "I'd be happy to do that, Ed."

As I left the office to comply with his request, I heaved a sigh of relief.

First Government Job

After Daniel and I passed the Civil Service Commission's examination (taken the day after our wedding) for a GS-4 position, we found out that a person had to have supervisory experience in order to be considered. The GS-4 position was one pay grade above the entry level, and no one I knew with supervisory experience would ever consider accepting a salary that low.

The following year I decided I would take the Civil Service Commission's entry-level examination even though it paid less than what I was earning.

When I took that examination, my typing score was excellent. The four years I spent typing constantly in my secretarial position proved that practice *does* make perfect.

I was told by a Civil Service Commission employee that I would receive only three job offers. If I did not accept one of them, my name would be removed from their register.

My first interview was with a supervisor employed by the Veterans Administration whose office was located at the Federal Center. I was thrilled because it would be close to home.

I don't recall being interviewed, but I vividly remember meeting the staff. It was someone's birthday, and everyone was taking a break to celebrate the occasion with coffee and cake. I was invited to join them.

As I ate my cake and sipped my coffee, I looked around the room. There were a dozen silent people with glum expressions on their faces, and I thought, 'If this is how they look while attending a party, I don't want to see them on a bad day!'

I declined the offer.

My next interview was with the supervisor at a Selective Service Administration office. They weren't at the Federal Center, but their location was much closer to home than the Plant.

I liked the woman who interviewed me, and the two other employees who worked there smiled at me.

I wasn't thrilled about the job, but I was afraid that my third, and final offer, would be in a place as bad as the Veterans Administration so I accepted the position.

I was correct about the supervisor and her two employees; they were very nice people. The older of the two employees was, however, a bit odd. She was from South Dakota, and several times each day, she would gaze listlessly out the window and say in her nasal voice, "One of these days, my ship will come in."

No one responded to her comment.

My biggest shock working in this office was the antiquated equipment. I was once again using a manual typewriter. The desk was old, and the only way I could open its center drawer was by putting my foot on the side drawer and bodily forcing it open.

The major challenge each day was staying in my typist's chair. It was wooden and swiveled and rolled in an acceptable fashion. Unfortunately, the spring that kept the seat level was broken. The only way I could keep myself from sliding off was by digging the heels of my shoes into the floor!

Pardon?

The first time I entered the Bureau of Mines Payroll Office was for my interview. I could not believe my eyes. It was a surreal scene.

Their office was located on the second floor of a wing which had been an add-on to the original building. It was constructed using metal-framed windows that were opened by pushing a metal rod out and propping it against the window frame. Some of the panes had been painted to cut down on glare, and there were no screens.

Another thing this office lacked was a ceiling. The wiring for the electrical outlets to operate the adding machines and typewriters came streaming down from a high beam in the rafters to a dozen desks where the employees worked.

They reminded me of the streamers my classmates and I had strung for a high school sock hop.

The interview went well, and the reason I accepted the position was because I could drive to and from work, in good weather, in five minutes.

After six months on the job, I no longer noticed our bizarre surroundings, and paid little attention to the occasional bird who flew in and perched on the rafters.

The women who worked there were not only nice, but the most hardworking, conscientious, and diligent people I had ever worked with. Without exception, everyone made certain that "their" employees got paid on time.

Our desks were in three rows across the room, with space in between. About six feet behind me sat Helen.

One morning, I turned my chair around and asked her about a problem I was having. She explained what I needed to do to correct it.

Before turning back to my desk, I said, "You know, Helen, Daniel says that I mumble."

She said, "Pardon?"

Open Mouth, Insert Foot

Throughout my life I have said things which I regret, but there were two incidents during my tenure with the Bureau of Mines that I have never forgotten.

The Federal Center awarded their concession stand contracts for the large buildings on its site to people who were legally blind. The stand in our building was operated by a very pleasant elderly gentleman.

One afternoon, I went to the stand to purchase a sugary treat to help get me through the remainder of the day. He was not there. I selected my favorite—a Snickers Bar—and waited.

When he returned, I said, "You certainly are a trusting soul to leave the stand unattended. I'd be afraid someone would rob me blind!"

*****

One winter day, I came to work wearing a black turtlenecked sweater and black slacks. I had finished checking my time sheets for accuracy and was taking them to the data entry office located on the first floor.

When I passed through the doorway leading to their area, I noticed a young Black man high on a ladder above me applying white paint to the wall.

As I looked up at him, I said, "Oh, be careful, I don't want to get white on my black!"

Hairdo

Sadly, in my working career, I only became well-acquainted with five African Americans, and one of them was my supervisor. His name was Norm.

Norm had retired from the Army after twenty years of service to our country. He was an excellent supervisor with a good sense of humor, and his afro haircut was always perfectly trimmed.

While working for Norm, my desk abutted an exterior wall with a window. The view was of a small parklike setting—grass, cottonwood trees, and a pond. The pond was frequented by mallard ducks.

Occasionally, I would see a pair of the ducks mate. The colorful drake would swim round and round and round the hen, and then he mounted her tail feathers. He was there no more than three seconds when his wings began to flap. He rose a few inches and then settled back down into the water. As he swam away, I was certain he had a smile on his beak.

After I'd worked for Norm a few months, I decided I needed a change. The change was going to be a new hair style. I made an appointment for the following weekend at my beauty salon where I requested a repeat of a style I had worn several times in the past. I liked the style because it was so easy to care for—no curlers required. When I returned to the office on Monday, I was sporting an afro.

When Norm saw me, he looked surprised and said, "Your hair looks just like mine."

"Yes, it does, but there's one big difference."

"What's that?"

"You got yours for free; mine cost fifty bucks!"

Sour Apple

The last job I had before becoming disabled was in a personnel office where I related this story to my five coworkers.

My parents had a crab apple tree in their front yard. Each spring, its white blossoms made it look like a gigantic popcorn ball. In the fall, it would be covered with tiny red fruit. They were beautiful to look at, but sour as swill.

This tree always provided Mom with enough fruit to make jelly that would see us through until the next year's crop ripened.

My sister, Luanne, and her three-year-old son, David, were at Mom's one day when the crab apples were at their peak.

David and I were outside, and I picked two apples. I kept one and handed the other to him.

I pretended to take a bite out of mine. As I did the mock bite and chewing, I said, "Mmmmmm. This is good. Mmmmmm. Give yours a try."

David took a *real* bite from his crab apple. His sweet little face contorted at the terrible taste of the fruit.

I laughed.

Without saying a word, he spat the crab apple onto the ground, looked daggers at me, and stomped toward the house.

He did not respond when I called to him, "I'm sorry, Sweetie."

My coworkers thought it was a funny story until my supervisor asked, "How old were you?"

"Nineteen."

"NINETEEN??!!! You should be ashamed of yourself!"

Everyone agreed.

They were right, of course. However, the truth is, if given the opportunity, I would probably do it again.

CHAPTER 4

DOCTORS

Family Physician

In the early seventies, I saw Dr. Hiroshi for the first time. He would be my primary care physician for the next thirty years. He was an excellent doctor who always referred me to top-notch specialists. Best of all, he had a sense of humor.

After seeing him for a few years, I asked, "Dr. Hiroshi, would it be alright if I called you Dr. H?"

His response was, "You can call me anything you want—just call me!"

*****

There are numerous family practice physicians who do not perform pelvic examinations. Dr. H was not one of them. Because of that, I faithfully scheduled my female exam at the same time each year.

Dr. H, his nurse and I were always ill at ease during this procedure. One year, I decided I would try to lighten things up.

I had purchased a sheet of tattoo decals, and one of them was a red devil complete with cape, horns and a long tail with a spade on its end. It was two inches tall.

The day before my scheduled pelvic exam, I applied the tattoo to my inner right thigh a few inches below my crotch.

In the office the following day, his nurse was getting me into position for the exam. You know the routine—"Further down, further down, once more. Okay, that's good." When she was putting my feet into the stirrups, she spotted my artwork.

"What's this?"

"It's a removable tattoo. Don't say anything to Doc. Let's surprise him."

With a grin on her face, she nodded in agreement. She placed the paper sheet over my knees which covered everything from the waist down. She opened the door a bit, and Dr. H entered.

He and I exchanged pleasantries while he put on his rubber gloves and glanced over the supplies making sure he had everything he needed to complete the procedure.

Dr. H was not a tall person, so when he sat down, his head was below the sheet covering my knees.

He lifted the bottom of the sheet. He stopped. He moved his head closer to my body. With his hand, he lowered the paper sheet between my knees, and, with a perplexed look on his face said, "What have you done?!"

"Don't you think he's a cute devil?"

No response.

"It's removable, Doc."

He shook his head back and forth, showing me the grin I had seen many times before—mission accomplished.

*****

Several years had passed since I had done anything "fun" at an appointment with Dr. H. My yearly physical was approaching, and I began to mentally form a plan.

Dr. H. always began my physical with the pelvic exam and then checked my other body parts and their functions. One of those tests was my reflexes. I had never had a good response when my reflexes were tested.

Dr. H. began by checking my wrists and elbows with his small red rubber-headed hammer. My reflexes reacted as they always did—not much movement. He then slid the paper sheet back and exposed my knees.

I lowered my head and focused my eyes on the testing area.

Dr. H put his hand on the top of my left knee and gently tapped the inside of it with the hammer.

My right foot twitched.

He repeated the procedure by tapping the outside of my left knee.

My right leg jumped up slightly. I could sense his disbelief, but he said nothing.

I kept looking down.

He walked around the table. He put his hand atop my right knee and gently tapped it on the inside.

My left foot twitched.

45

He repeated the process by tapping the outside of the right knee.

My left leg jumped up.

He stepped back. I could feel his eyes boring into the top of my skull.

I didn't lift my head, but I raised my eyes and looked at him.

As soon as our eyes met, I burst into laughter.

He smiled and shook his head. "What am I going to do with you?"

Where's My Bite?

My father lost his teeth when he was in his early forties because of gum disease. My entire life I heard him say, "Do whatever you can to save your teeth."

Going to the dentist in our family was not a routine thing. Dental care was costly and having a roof over our heads and food to eat was far more important.

When I was in my early teens, Mom decided it was time to have my teeth examined. She took me to a dentist in a nearby town.

I was terrified of dentists. The mere sound of the drill made me break out in a cold sweat. Dr. Lomont's waiting room had a large aquarium containing beautifully colored fish. I watched them intently trying to keep myself calm until it was my turn in the chair.

For me, the worst part of going to a dentist was the Novocain shots. Once I'd passed that threshold, I was okay.

On my first visit, the dentist found sixteen cavities! I crossed many thresholds that year getting my teeth repaired.

Once again, the laxness in dental checkups returned.

When I married in my early twenties, my husband, Daniel, was in the habit of seeing his dentist once a year for cleaning and checkup. I followed suit.

In my early thirties, I noticed that I was no longer able to bite sewing thread in two with my front teeth. A few months later, the first upper left molar began to turn sideways!

I made an appointment with our dentist; he had no idea what was happening.

When I mentioned my predicament to a coworker, she suggested that I make an appointment to see her dentist. I did.

Dr. Dickey gave me a thorough checkup. While pushing my cheeks back, he instructed me to bite, click and grind my teeth. This method gave him a full view of what was happening. He then took numerous X-rays.

When the exam was complete, he said, "You have a malformed palate, a cross bite, tongue thrusting and bone loss."

I was too stunned to speak.

He continued, "My recommendation is that you see a periodontist. If he thinks your jawbones would be strong enough, we could do the preparation work for you to get braces."

My mouth was hanging open. I had difficulty comprehending what he had just said. The thoughts racing through my mind were, 'I hate dental work; there will be frequent pain; it will cost a great deal of money.'

"I'm going to have to think about this."

"That's fine," he responded. "If you have any questions, give me a call."

For several days, I thought of little else. I had two choices. I could do as he suggested, or I could try to find a dentist who would remove my teeth and make me a set of dentures.

Having either of those procedures was very upsetting, but I kept hearing my father say, "Do whatever you have to do to keep your own teeth."

I called Dr. Dickey and agreed to his plan.

My first stop was at the periodontist's office. He did a thorough examination and decided that my jawbone would tolerate the stress of braces after one surgical procedure. I scheduled the appointment.

On the appointed day, I went in and had the roots of my four upper front teeth "deep" cleaned. Not only did I get Novocain shots to numb the area, but his assistant laid a rubber hose with an opening facing downward across the bridge of my nose. That opening allowed the gas it expelled to enter my nostrils.

The procedure began when the doctor slit my gums and began scraping the exposed roots. At that moment, my gas inhalation increased greatly. One deep breath was followed by others.

After the scraping was compete, the gums were stitched back together and a protective cream-colored claylike compound was applied to the gums over the stitches. This would remain in place until the gums were healed.

By this time, the gas inhalation had made me feel light-headed.

When the doctor said to his assistant, "Pass me the dip," I responded with, "Who's got the chips?"

With a nod from the doctor, his assistant turned off the gas supply.

Phase two of Dr. Dickey's plan was the extraction of the four small teeth behind the eye teeth on the upper gum and the canine teeth on the lower jawbone. I returned to his office for this procedure.

He had given me the choice of having the four teeth extracted in two separate appointments or having them extracted all at the same time. Since I had never experienced an extraction, I opted to have it done in one appointment—get it over with quickly.

When Daniel and I arrived for the appointment, Dr. Dickey's assistant took me to a room and placed the bib over my chest. The doctor came in and gave me the Novocain shots.

As my mouth began to numb, I started to experience a strange sensation. Having my entire mouth deadened was a new experience, and I realized that I could not feel myself swallowing, if indeed, I *was* swallowing.

I felt like I was strangling and went into panic mode.

His assistant's quiet, calming words and the fact that she was holding my left hand while applying a cold compress to my forehead with her other hand, I managed to keep myself under control.

When I was completely calm, Dr. Dickey began.

It went like this with the first three teeth. Clamp onto the tooth with the extractor and twist. That action produced a loud "crunching" sound. Pull on the extractor. That action produced a "popping" sound.

When the extraction of the fourth tooth was in progress, Dr. Dickey said aloud, "Damn!"

His exclamation made my eyebrows shoot up. I thought, 'Damn! That doesn't sound good.'

"I'm sorry, Diane," he said. "That root has broken off. I'm going to have to cut your gum to get it out. Will you be all right?"

I nodded in the affirmative.

It didn't take long to remove the root and required only two stitches. In the ensuing years, when I was in his office, I never again heard him use profanity.

With the preliminary work accomplished, it was now time to get the braces.

Dr. Bruce was my orthodontist, and I was, at age thirty-six, unique compared to his usual patients. The first time I entered his reception area, I saw numerous teenagers. Most of them were accompanied by a parent. Once I had checked in and sat down, I hoped the newcomers would think I was waiting for my child.

When Dr. Bruce glued the bands to my teeth, it was not painful, but the odor of the adhesive was noxious. Once the bands were affixed, he quickly and adeptly wound, twisted and tightened the wire around the hooks on the bands. I experienced a few gentle stabs from the wire's ends during the process. After cutting off each wire to the correct length, he tucked its end back under the affixed wires to protect my mouth from constant stabbings.

Once everything was in place, it didn't seem too uncomfortable. 'Perhaps,' I thought, 'it won't be as bad as people say.'

The rude awakening came when I began chewing the food I had prepared for dinner. It felt as if I had barbed wire inside my mouth. After eating, my cheeks and tongue felt like they had become raw meat.

Every night at bedtime, for the first week, I placed rolled up facial tissues between the braces and my cheeks to give my mouth a few hours of relief. After several weeks my cheeks and tongue had toughened up, and I was able to eat comfortably.

Periodically, the old wires were removed and replaced with new ones. The process of having new wires attached involved Dr. Bruce placing my head into various wrestling holds—the most frequently used hold was the half-nelson. Since he was a barrel-chested man, I just relaxed and enjoyed the comfort of his soft, warm chest.

There was no pain on the day of the tightening, but the following morning was another story. The added pressure on the teeth caused so much pain that I could not touch my upper and lower teeth together for three days. This process was repeated month after month for three and a half years.

When I was two years into this process, Daniel and I had my parents down for a cookout to celebrate Father's Day.

We were sitting on the patio having drinks when my father asked, "Why did you have those braces put on?"

"Because you told me to always do whatever it took to save my own teeth."

"I didn't mean to go *that* far!"

"*Now* you tell me!"

The "Hyst" Heist

In my early teens, I worried there was something wrong because I did not begin menstruating until I was sixteen. I was fortunate in that I had a light flow and experienced only moderate cramping two days prior and on the first day of my period.

I always felt that menstruating was my womanly duty and adjusted to its inconveniences.

When I was in my thirty-eighth year, I began having "female" problems. The menstrual cramps began earlier and earlier prior to my flow. During the following year, it had reached the point that the only time I was *not* cramping was the last three days of my period.

I consulted Dr. H and he referred me to Dr. Finn—a gynecologist. I scheduled an appointment with him.

One always expects to be kept waiting at a doctor's office, but Dr. Finn's office had a unique system. Upon arrival at the appointed time, I signed in at the reception desk and sat down to wait. Eventually, a woman called my name and took me to another room that looked similar to the one I had just left. She told me to be seated and that someone would soon be with me.

This area had several women I had seen in the reception area.

Again, I waited. Later, another woman came in and took me to a smaller room across the hall. I hoped I was making progress.

"The nurse will be in soon," she said.

'Surely,' I thought, 'that was a good sign.'

After another wait, the nurse *did* come in. She sat with me and asked questions and filled out a form with my responses.

She stood. I thought, 'Another wait?'

"Come with me." I gave a silent sigh of relief and followed her down the hall and into a spacious, well-appointed office.

Pointing to a chair facing the desk, she said, "Sit here. The doctor will be with you soon."

I wasn't sure I believed her.

A few minutes later, Dr. Finn walked in and introduced himself. I was finally in the presence of the physician. It didn't take long to determine that this man was condescending, pompous, and truly enamored with himself.

I was disappointed, but kept reminding myself that he must be an excellent physician or Dr. H. would not have recommended him.

I followed the doctor to another room where he examined me. My uterus had fibroid growths. Because of my age, he decided that a vaginal hysterectomy was the best option. His staff scheduled the surgery.

The afternoon before the day of the surgery, Daniel drove me to the hospital. I checked in at the admissions desk and was then escorted to the lab.

I had been scheduled for a urine test and a blood draw. There was a time when giving a urine sample was easy, but things had changed. The doctors began asking for a midstream sample.

The suggested procedure went like this: Urinate a little. Stop. Urinate to fill the cup. Stop. Place cup on counter. Complete urination.

I don't know about other females, but when I begin to urinate, stopping the flow is next to impossible. I tried following their instructions a couple of times but failed miserably.

From that point on, I used my own method. I sat on the toilet placing the specimen cup between my legs next to the front of the bowl.

I began to urinate. When I thought it was at midstream, I moved the cup into the flow. Not being able to see how full the cup was, the urine overflowed and got onto my fingers. I moved the cup to front of bowl and finished urinating. I then emptied the cup to the desired quantity, sat it on the counter and stood up.

When clothed, I washed my hands, placed the lid on the urine-filled cup and ran water over the entire container and dried it with a paper towel. I then washed and rinsed my hands two additional times. What a task!

After turning in my specimen, I was escorted to a chair for the blood draw. Just the thought of giving blood always made me feel nauseous and faint. I watched as the nurse prepared me for the procedure. When she reached for the needle, I looked the other way until the task was completed.

From there I was taken to my room on the sixth floor. When I entered the room, I stopped dead in my tracks.

"This is a private room. My insurance won't pay for this."

"It's the only one available," the nurse said, "so you'll be charged the price of a double."

"That's great!" Crossing to the window, I added, "And look at that view!" The Rockies looked spectacular against the fall blue sky.

She handed me the infamous "it's drafty up your back-side gown" and motioned that I change in the bathroom. I did.

After hanging my clothes in the closet, I climbed into bed.

I noticed the nurse had opened my plastic "kit," consisting of the foot bath tub, kidney-shaped dish (hoped that wouldn't be needed), toothpaste, toothbrush, tiny plastic glass and a large drawstring plastic bag.

What the nurse didn't know was that my paternal cousin was a urologist, and it was his idea to have this array of items in one compact package. His manufacturing company produced them, and it made him a wealthy man.

Next item on the agenda was selecting from their menu. I don't remember what I chose, but I do remember thinking that the food was good—for institutional fare.

Mid-afternoon, a young woman came in rolling a large cart with testing equipment sitting on its top shelf. The apparatus sported numerous dials and a long plastic hose. I wondered where that hose would be inserted.

The technician was a tall, thin girl wearing an excessive amount of make-up, and she had the longest fingernails I had ever seen. My first thought was that the bright red nails were glued on. A closer examination changed my mind. Her nails curved down like an eagle's talons and were definitely homegrown.

She was a cheerful, knowledgeable person. While she was explaining the machine's function, she said, "The pulmonary function test is to determine the amount of air that you can rapidly expel from your lungs."

In other words, they wanted to know how much "puff" I possessed. Having smoked for more than two decades, I thought, 'I'm going to flunk!'

The test of my exhaling ability was done twice in quick succession. With each exhale I made, I felt decidedly light-headed.

To my surprise—and relief—I had passed within the acceptable range.

In the late afternoon, another young nurse arrived. She was the barber. Since I had never had my genitalia shaved, I was apprehensive—and embarrassed. The nurse seemed uncomfortable, too, but performed the task in a professional manner.

I had no idea what the appropriate conversation would be in this situation, but I decided to give it a try.

"How long have you been a nurse?"

"Three years."

"Is this the only job that you do?"

"If it *was*, I'd quit!"

When I was alone, I took a peek at my haircut. The nurse had shaved the lower two-thirds and left the top one-third untouched. My labia had bangs!

After a liquid supper, I laid back and was enjoying a television program.

An older nurse came in, and in a cheerful voice said, "Time for your enema!"

'Dread of dreads,' I thought. I had taken only a couple of enemas in my life because of constipation desperation. Enemas made me nauseous, and I had no anal holding power.

The nurse filled the pitcher with warm water. The granules she added turned it milky white. The pitcher had an attached hose with a pincher shut off.

As she approached the bed, she said, "I will insert the hose into your rectum and release some of this liquid. I want you to hold it as long as you can. Okay?"

"Okay."

She began the procedure.

As soon as she removed the tube, I said, "I've got to go!" and made a mad dash to the toilet.

As I passed her, she said, "Hold it as long as you can!"

When I sat on the toilet, there was an instant whoosh.

She was standing in the doorway. I sheepishly looked up at her. "I'll try to do better next time." It was obvious she had her doubts.

I returned to the bed. The remainder of the fluid was inserted and the tube removed.

I laid there clinching my rectum as tightly as I could. Clinching my teeth seemed to help, too. I could feel the fluid moving higher and higher into my colon. I felt nauseous and light-headed.

The nurse was watching me closely. I managed a forced smile.

"Why don't you head to the bathroom? Keep holding it as long as you can."

I sat up, slid off the bed, walked stiff-legged to the toilet, and sat down carefully.

"You did well that time!"

I was relieved—in more ways than one.

The following morning, I was awakened bright and early. I was now in the total fasting phase.

Nurses came in and out doing the final preparations. One hour prior to the surgery, I was given a pill which was supposed to relax me and cause some grogginess. It had no effect. I felt bright-eyed and bushy-tailed.

Next came the insertion of the long needle into the back of my right hand to which an IV tube was attached. These items were taped securely in place.

Shortly after that, two young orderlies of the male persuasion came in, and with instructions from the nurse, gingerly transferred me onto the gurney. The IV tubing and needle were checked. Everything was A-OK.

The young men maneuvered me gently through the door and out into the hallway. Once we had a straight, clear path, the pace picked up.

Watching the overhead neon lights zip past was fun. They did, of course, slow down for corners and for the entry into and the exit from the elevator. Upon reaching our final destination, they gently pushed me through the double doors and "parked" me in the surgical waiting area.

I rested undisturbed for a while. When I glanced to my left, I saw Dr. H. He was going to assist in the surgery.

As he approached, I smiled broadly and raised my left hand. He took hold of it.

"I'm so glad you're here, Doc. You're the only one at this party I know!"

He smiled. "I'm going to go and change now. Don't worry. Everything will be fine."

His presence and the sound of his voice always had a calming effect on me.

When the surgical theater had been readied for my operation, I was wheeled in. Dr. H, Dr. Finn, the anesthesiologist, and several other staff members wearing white were standing in their respective positions.

I was transferred to the operating table, maneuvered into the correct position, and secured in place with adjustable straps. The anesthesiologist attached his equipment to my IV. I looked at the ceiling as the final preparations were made. I was impressed by the huge surgical light.

A rack was placed just above my shoulders and fabric was draped over it so that my view was blocked.

There was a loud crash. It sounded as if a cart containing operating tools and other paraphernalia had been knocked over.

My first thought was, 'STAPH INFECTION!!!'

Then—nothing.

The next thing I remember was my gurney's wheels bumping over the door guides as I exited the elevator on the sixth floor.

I had survived.

I am now a statistic.

One Hemorrhoid

After having severe hemorrhoid pain for weeks, I made an appointment with Dr. H. When he looked at my rectum, he said, "I don't see anything."

Using a fingernail, I indicated the location.

He brought his head closer, "Oh, yes, I see. It's very tiny."

"I've been using Preparation H, but it's not helping."

"I want you to see a proctologist." He recommended the same doctor who had done Daniel's hemorrhoid surgery—Dr. Bernard.

I had seen Dr. Bernard once. He was leaving Daniel's hospital room after a post-op visit. I thought he was a plumber.

I called and scheduled an appointment.

Dr. Bernard had no problem seeing my teeny, tiny hemorrhoid.

"I'll be able to remove that here in the office," he said. "Just make an appointment on your way out."

I liked Dr. Bernard, and considering the artwork on his walls, it was obvious he had a sense of humor.

One of the bathroom walls had a large framed picture of a little boy with a bare bottom, sitting on a jetty with his puppy next to him enjoying a day of fishing, and the examining room had a Picasso pen-and-ink print which depicted a person's buttock using only a few strokes of his pen.

On the day of the hemorrhoid removal, I arrived at the office early. I signed in, got a magazine, and sat down. The office was full—not one empty seat.

Knowing I was going to experience pain, I was too nervous to read. I held the magazine in front of my face to give the impression I was reading, but lowered it just enough so that I could peer over its top.

Just as I did this, screaming came from the back area. Everyone was as shocked as I was.

A male voice was yelling, "Nooooooo! Don't do it! Oh, my god! You're killing me! No! No! Stop! Stop! Pleeeeeease stop!"

As I scanned the faces in the waiting room, it was obvious which people were the patients and which ones came along for the ride. We patients had beads of sweat on our foreheads.

Shortly after the screaming ended, a man of slight stature who was accompanied by a woman holding his arm, came into the waiting room and quickly exited.

I was the next patient to be called. I bravely followed the nurse into the room where I had the initial examination. I disrobed as instructed by the nurse and was lying on my left side when Dr. Bernard entered. We exchanged pleasantries.

I asked, "Why was that man screaming?"

"Men are such babies! They can't tolerate the least little pain."

I now knew that I had to be especially brave—and quiet.

The numbing shots required a lot of teeth clenching. Once numbed, I relaxed a little.

When Dr. Bernard made the tiny cut, he said to his nurse, "I didn't expect so much blood. Get more gauze." She complied.

Over my right shoulder, and in a calm voice, I said, "Did I forget to mention that I'm a hemophiliac?"

"WHAT?!!!"

I quickly added, "Sorry, Doc. Bad joke!"

<u>Mental Images</u>

My sister, Luanne, and I were both cursed with mental image flashes. When someone told either of us about an experience they had had, we instantly visualized it in our mind's eye. For me, it's like watching a movie.

I don't know about Luanne, but my movies sometime took on the characteristics of the Key Stone Cops or a cartoon.

We have both laughed out loud at inappropriate moments because of what we are "seeing."

My best case in point occurred when I was in my dentist's office.

Dr. Flowers was a very serious man and had told me more than once that he was modest. During one of my visits, we were discussing professional massages.

He said, "My masseuse is blind."

I burst into hysterical laughter. He looked shocked and puzzled.

"I'm sorry, Doc. I just got a mental image of a man wearing dark glasses coming into the room bumping into things, and feeling around trying to determine where to start!"

My sense of humor was lost on him.

He responded in a serious, sincere voice, "Someone always brings him into the room and orients him."

I choked back laughter and managed to say, "Of course they do."

Breast Augmentation

Step 1

From a young age, I thought femininity was based on a woman's cleavage. After going through puberty, I had none. My itty-bitty breasts were smaller than a double A cup.

When I was in high school, I walked stooped forward with my books held close to my body to hide the fact that I was flat-chested. For years, I was able to identify myself to others as a female by wearing dangling earrings.

When I was forty-four years old, I had been disabled and housebound for two years, and there was no hope that my health would ever improve.

When my self-esteem was at its lowest ebb, I began trying to figure out what I could do to improve it. While watching television one afternoon, breast implants were the topic being discussed. For the next year, I mulled over the pros and cons of having that surgical procedure.

I decided that I would need to have a similar traumatic experience in order to find out how, in my condition, I would tolerate it. Eight months into the thinking process, my two upper left front teeth reached the point that I could flip them back and forth with a fingertip.

I wondered, 'Could this be the test?'

Step 2

I called my periodontist and scheduled an appointment. I asked Dr. Deel to recommend a dentist who would be willing to extract my two left front teeth.

He understood why his patients eventually reached the point that they no longer wanted to fight their tooth, gum and bone loss problems.

In response to my request, he recommended Dr. Heeps. He was semi-retired, but Dr. Deel was certain he would help me. I called and made an appointment for a consultation.

Dr. Heeps and his wife, Rosemary, who was his receptionist and dental assistant, were wonderful people. They were warm and caring and both had an excellent sense of humor.

When I had been seated in the dental chair, Dr. Heeps' first response to my request was a gentle nudge to my upper right arm and a suggestion that I keep my teeth.

When I explained my dental history and my physical condition, he agreed to do what I had requested. He made dental impressions, and I scheduled an appointment for the extractions.

When Daniel and I arrived, we were the only ones in the waiting room. Pleasantries were exchanged with Rosemary. She guided me into a different room than I had been in during my first visit. I sat down in the chair; she put on my bib. Dr. Heeps joined us.

As he was making final preparations, I glanced to my left. Attached to the spit bowl and traveling to the nearest drill was a dust web. My mind raced as I adjusted myself in the chair.

Dr. Heeps was ready. He stood before me with the Novocain-filled syringe in hand. I immediately closed my eyes and opened my mouth. He gave me several shots. I heaved a sigh of relief when he finished. I was ready to relax while the numbing medication took effect.

Just as I had made myself comfortable in the chair, Dr. Heeps was in front of me holding the extracting tool. When his hand came toward my face, I forcibly grabbed his wrist. My heart was racing.

"Don't you think you should give it more time to numb?"

"It will be fine. Trust me."

I released his wrist and opened my mouth.

He put the extractor on a tooth. I heard, *crunch, pop.* He placed the tooth on the tray. He repeated the action with the other tooth. Once again, *crunch, pop.* Now there were two of my teeth on the tray.

I had felt nothing.

The blood was absorbed with cotton rolls. He held an acrylic partial plate with two left front teeth attached close to my exposed gum. He took the appliance to his work area, and I heard grinding. Upon his return, he removed the cotton and placed the appliance into my mouth.

It was an unbelievable fit. The sockets where the teeth had been removed were filled perfectly with the acrylic teeth. It was impossible to tell that my two front teeth had been removed.

I scheduled my next appointment, and Daniel and I headed for home. I glanced down at my watch. The entire procedure had taken thirty minutes.

Dr. Heeps was correct—he was trustworthy. He was also the most skilled denture dentist I would ever encounter.

Since I had tolerated this procedure without any serious consequences, I decided it was time to begin the next step.

Step 3

At my next scheduled appointment with Dr. H, I broached the subject. "Dr. H, I've been thinking about having my breasts enlarged."

"Why do you want to do that?!"

"So I will feel feminine."

"Is this Daniel's idea?"

"No. He doesn't want me to do it."

He looked thoughtful for a few moments. In a calm, quiet voice, he said, "Are you sure about this?"

"Yes, I am."

"Dr. Nelson is the plastic surgeon I would recommend."

Step 4

I scheduled an appointment. The first thing Dr. Nelson asked me was, "Why do you want to have the breast augmentation surgery done?"

"My entire life I have based femininity on the amount of cleavage a woman has. I've never had any. I just want to feel feminine."

He smiled. "Okay." He headed for the door saying, "Disrobe from the waist up."

I followed his instructions and sat myself on edge of the examining table.

When he returned, he walked over to where I was seated and scanned my breasts with his eyes. He then put a hand on the outside of each breast and pushed them toward one another.

"I think we can get you some cleavage." We both smiled.

He helped me from the table and asked me to stand with my back close to the wall across the room.

"I always take a before and after photograph." He got a Polaroid camera, moved into position, and took the picture.

When it developed, I was surprised. I thought it would be only of my breasts; instead, it was from the waist up. I was slouching!

I redressed, and we continued with the consultation.

He told me what his fee would be and explained, "I charge large amounts for the elective surgeries so that I can hold down the costs for people with deformities and those who have been disfigured in accidents."

I agreed with his policy.

He continued, "There are many things that can go wrong with breast augmentation surgery. I want you to read this, and if you still want the surgery, I'll have you sign a release form."

He handed me a sheet of paper. It was filled from top to bottom and side to side—no margins—on both sides of the page in small print. It listed anything and everything from the prostheses rupturing to its ability to cause a rare form of cancer.

I signed the release form.

The procedure would be done at a surgical center rather than the hospital. As the center was located closer to home, I found that quite acceptable. In addition, the procedure would not be scheduled until my check for his services had cleared my bank and was deposited into his account.

I agreed to this, too.

"I think," he said, "that I would like to use a prosthesis that is placed under the muscle. You're a thin person which works well with this prosthesis. There is one drawback."

"What's that?"

"Since the muscle will be stretched, it will be more painful."

I thought, 'Surely, it won't be that bad. After all, I had withstood the double tooth extractions.'

I responded, "I think it will be all right."

With that consent, he went to a cabinet and brought back a box.

"Let me show you one."

Inside the box was a pristine prosthesis. It had a pouch of silicone about one-half inch thick. Attached to that was loose, clear, heavy-duty plastic. He pulled a tube attached to the loose plastic until it was straight.

"This is how the saline solution will enter the prostheses. I'll fill it until the desired size is reached and then I'll close it off."

"How big will you make them?" I asked, as I gestured a foot away from my chest with my hands.

He laughed. "Not *that* big! Actually, I won't make them too large for your frame. I don't do that."

"I'll trust your judgment. I'm sure they will be perfect."

Step 5

I sent a check for the total cost of the procedure to Dr. Nelson. Ten days later, I received a call and scheduled the date of my surgery. When the day arrived, Daniel took me to the surgical center. I spent time in the waiting room filling out and signing forms.

When I was taken into the surgical area, I became more relaxed. My nurse had had her breasts enhanced and offered much appreciated encouragement and advice. She was delighted with her results.

The anesthesiologist came in and inserted the IV. He was a soft-spoken man with warm hands. He explained exactly what would occur during the surgical procedure.

At the appointed time, I was wheeled into the operating room. The anesthesiologist was there and two other people I didn't recognize. Everyone was busy.

Dr. Nelson came in and stood beside the table. He took hold of my left hand. Smiling down at me, he said, "Are you ready?"

I gripped his hand tightly, "Will you promise me something?"

"What is it?"

"If you drop something, will you promise that you won't pick it up?"

Everyone in the room laughed out loud.

Dr. Nelson held my hand in both of his, "I promise."

I heaved a sigh of relief. Smiling up at him, I said, "I'm ready."

My next conscious thought was, 'I don't think I'll have the surgery.' I felt the pain and thought, 'Too late!'

A few moments later someone took hold of my shoulders and shook me hard. She yelled, *"DIANE! WAKE UP!"*

I thought, 'Why is she yelling? I'm right here.' I opened my eyes.

In a normal, pleasant voice, she said, "There you are. Welcome back."

I was perplexed by her remark, but smiled and said, "Thank you."

On the way home, Daniel told me that I hadn't regained consciousness in the normal time frame which had caused anxiety among the nursing staff. I was given a shot, but continued sleeping soundly. That was when the "brute force" tactics began.

My dental pain "test" turned out to be laughable. The pain I experienced after the surgery was sometimes so severe that it took my breath away. I had failed to consider the result of stretching my chest muscles over half a cantaloupe.

It was strange having large breasts sitting on my chest. When lying down, it seemed that I had to look over their tops or through the newly created valley to see my feet.

The first time I sat at the kitchen table and reached across my plate for the fork, my upper arm brushed against my breast. I felt as though I had gotten fresh with myself, and actually said aloud, "Pardon me!"

The first three days after the surgery were the worst. During that time, I could not move my arms away from my body without causing severe pain. After that, I began to recover, and little by little, I was able to move my arms in all directions.

My intervening appointments with Dr. Nelson went well.

On the day of my final visit, Daniel and I entered the elevator of Dr. Nelson's building along with another gentleman. We were going to the third floor; he to the fourth. We stood parallel to one another across the back of the car. I was in the middle.

I was wearing my large Air Force gray sunglasses which prevented anyone from seeing my eyes. Each of us appeared to be looking straight ahead following the progress of the ascending elevator.

Keeping my head straight, I looked to my left at our fellow passenger. He was looking out the corner of his right eye directly at my breasts. That was a first for me!

I know a tiny grin appeared at my lip edges, but I was able to subdue the riotous laughter I wanted to expel. As soon as we exited the elevator, a smile from ear to ear covered my face. I liked having a chest that someone noticed.

When I went into the examining room, I stripped from the waist up.

Dr. Nelson entered the room, "I see you're ready for your after photo."

"I am."

He got the camera; I positioned myself in the photographing area. This time I stood up straight and sucked in my tummy. Dr. Nelson took the picture.

My new breasts were lovely. He had given me the perfect size for my frame *and* the number and letter I had always coveted—36-B.

I went to the mirror and placing a hand on the outside of each breast, I pushed them toward the center. They did not touch.

"Dr. Nelson, I still don't have any cleavage."

"I can make them larger, but I can't relocate them."

We both laughed.

Not only do my augmented breasts make me feel feminine, they also provide me with entertainment.

When I stand in front of the mirror with my arms at my side and breasts bared, I say, "Ready to come to attention, girls? Okay, here we go. TENNN-HUT!!!"

When the ten-hut is uttered, I flex my chest muscles and my breasts follow orders. They "jump" to attention.

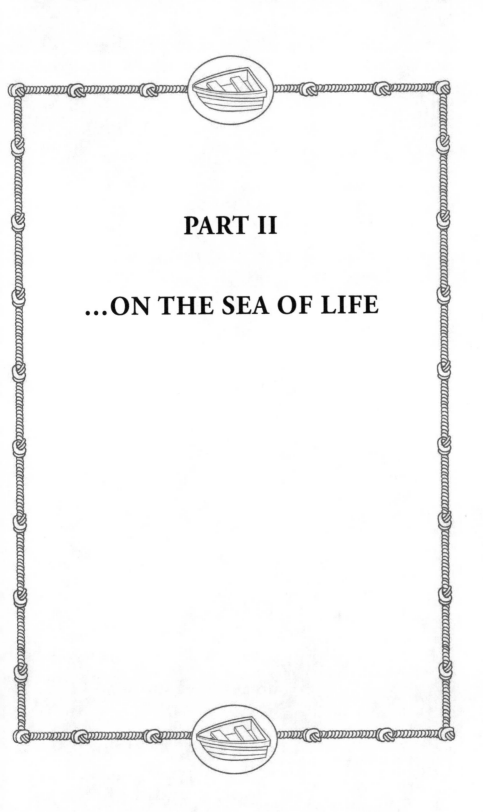

PART II

...ON THE SEA OF LIFE

CHAPTER 1

MYALGIC ENCEPHALOMYELITIS

I don't know if I was born with myalgic encephalo-myelitis, but I do remember the first time I experienced its symptoms.

I was three years old. I got up that morning wearing my flannel pajamas and went to the kitchen carrying my teddy bear in my left hand. I told Mama I felt terrible.

For some reason unbeknownst to me, she had the camera in her hand. She kept following me round and round the kitchen wanting me to pose for a picture.

I kept telling her now badly I felt, but she ignored me.

Feeling completely exhausted, I put my right forearm against the door frame and put my face on it to shield me from the camera and began crying.

She took the picture.

Everyone else thought it was a darling photo. Each time I saw it, tears came to my eyes because I remembered how badly I had felt.

That was the only time in my life Mama was cruel to me—albeit unintentional.

*****

When I was growing up, the only time a family member went to see a doctor was when a bone was broken or stitches were required. All other medical problems were treated with home remedies.

In November of my fourth-grade year, my first bout of myalgic encephalomyelitis began. The first symptom I experienced was my inability to go to sleep when I went to bed. It upset me so badly that I cried myself to sleep for weeks.

I finally accepted the fact that I would be awake for thirty minutes to one hour before sleep would arrive. I tried to convince myself to relax and think of pleasant things to pass the time. I told myself I might not be asleep, but I *was* resting, and that, in itself, was a good thing.

During that year, I experienced aches and pains throughout my entire body. I periodically ran a temperature and had bouts of vomiting and diarrhea. The worst part was the excessive fatigue. It helped when Mom changed my bedtime from 9:00 p.m. to 8:00 p.m.

Because I was missing so much school, Mom talked to my teacher. She gave Mom my homework so that I would not fall behind my classmates.

In retrospect, I'm grateful that I managed to pass the fourth grade—*and* learn my times tables through the tens.

The medical problems continued through the following summer and into the beginning of my fifth-grade year. In November of that year, I felt as though a switch inside me had been flipped. I felt normal again!

The only problem that remained was the insomnia. It became a permanent part of my life.

*****

During my senior year in high school, when I was seventeen, I began sleeping twelve hours on the nights I didn't have to attend classes. The worst part was, when I awoke, I was more tired than when I had gone to bed.

I was a cheerleader that year—in a *very* small school. That activity required an inordinate amount of physical exertion. The uniforms we wore were made of wool. I did all right during football season because we were outside in the fresh air. Basketball season was a different story.

Our gymnasium was small. When it was filled to capacity, it became exceedingly hot. Between the exertion and the heat, there were several times when I felt as though I was going to faint.

For the first time, Mom took me to see our family physician about my problems. He ran every test available at the time trying to determine the cause. He was very disappointed and genuinely concerned when he could not find an answer.

*****

For the next two decades, I periodically went to doctors in hopes of finding a cause for my health problems. The results were always the same. Tests were done; nothing was found. The doctor's responses varied from concerned to condescending to downright insulting.

It reached the point that when I developed a new symptom, I refused to see a doctor because I knew nothing would be found, and I didn't want to run the risk of being called a hypochondriac—or worse.

I had always done what my brain wanted my body to do rather than listening to what my body was telling me to do—rest, rest, rest. Inside my head, I was a dynamo with boundless energy and endless stamina. The fact that my body disagreed made me frustrated and angry.

For these reasons, I pushed myself on and on and on. When I reached the point I began crying for no reason, I knew I *had* to rest. My remedy was taking a nap in the afternoon and telling myself that would be sufficient. This routine went on for years.

When I was thirty-nine, I had a hysterectomy. After the surgery, I developed a minor infection and my health became worse. Over the next three years, I progressively became more and more fatigued. It was like living in a nightmare that I could not wake up from.

Midway through my shower on workday mornings, I had to lie down in the tub to rest before I could muster the strength to stand up and finish. I eventually changed my work schedule to part-time, and began coming home for lunch so I could lie down and rest before going back to the office to finish the day's work.

Three years after the hysterectomy, I caught a cold in the late summer which settled in my bronchial tubes. I went to Dr. H, and he prescribed medication. I called him twice to let him know there had been no improvement. He assured me it was a virus, and that I would get better. It would just take a little longer.

After six weeks, I made another appointment. When Dr. H walked into the examining room, I said, "It's *not* the cold. It's *not* the cough. There is something wrong inside of me!"

He recommended a specialist.

When I met Dr. Norman for the first time, Daniel was with me. He asked me the usual questions about my medical history, and then asked if I had been out of the country, come into contact with exotic birds (parrots or cockatoos), been exposed to mononucleosis or experienced any prolonged stress.

I answered "no" to each inquiry. The response was true except to the last question—prolonged stress. Being married to Daniel had caused me daily stress for nineteen years, but with him sitting next to me, I did not have the courage to tell Dr. Norman the truth.

When the question-and-answer segment ended, I was taken to an examining room where I disrobed—except for my panties. The usual paper sheet covered me from the waist down, and I was given a paper bolero and told to put the opening in the front.

Dr. Norman entered the room and began the examination. When he checked my breasts, he didn't open the top; he examined them covered.

"I don't embarrass easily," I said.

His response was, "I do!"

After the exam, I dressed and went to his lab where several vials of blood were drawn.

On my second visit, I was seated in his consultation room. Dr. Norman began telling me about a condition called Chronic Epstein-Barre Virus Syndrome (CEBV). He told me that if I recovered within one year, I would be fine. If I did not, the condition could be permanent. The only treatment was bed rest.

Being the eternal optimist, I chose to believe I would be well in one year.

At that time, I did not equate what I had experienced in the fourth grade as having anything to do with what was happening now. That epiphany occurred years later.

I spent the next year lying in bed or on the couch. I didn't have the strength to stay in an upright position for more than twenty minutes. Walking the thirty feet from the bedroom to the kitchen took so much strength that I had to lie flat on the floor and rest before I could sit up at the table and eat. On better days, I managed to finish a meal. Other days, I had to lie on the floor halfway through the meal and rest before I could return to the table and finish eating. I always rested on the floor after the meal before returning to bed.

The only time I left the house was for medical or dental appointments. Their venues were fifteen-minute drives from home. I would lie down in the car going both ways and hoped I could muster enough strength to stay upright until the appointment was completed.

When eleven months had passed, I had not improved. In fact, I had become worse.

I had slept only two or three hours each night for a week. At the same time, I experienced stomach pain and nausea to the point that I could not eat. After losing six pounds, I called Dr. H.

He prescribed a sleeping pill. The stomach problems disappeared, and with the aid of the pills, I was able to sleep six or seven hours each night.

With the knowledge I was not going to be well in one year, I began to grieve for the life I had lost.

First came the anger dressed in the "why me?" garb.

That was followed by sadness which caused endless crying.

Finally, there was acceptance.

This was my new life. I had to make the best of it. Knowing what I needed to do and doing it were two different things.

I felt as though I was on a stage surrounded by the people in my life. They had parts to play and lines to say. I had no part—no lines. I was simply there. This was the first time I considered suicide.

I began to mentally withdraw into my own fantasy world. In it, I was healthy, active, and productive. There were no problems—no stress. It was a wonderful place to be. For the next eight months, I spent ninety percent of my waking hours in my "special" place.

The following spring, I still had enough sanity left to realize that if I did not find something in reality to focus on, I would find myself in a mental institution.

Daniel had purchased a used upright piano. When he was a teenager, he had taken lessons and still had his beginner's book from the 1940s.

My mother's family was musical, and Mom could play the piano by "ear." I had learned a bit about the keyboard from her. I could play the first few bars of "Chop Sticks" and the scale notes properly from middle C to high C.

On my forty-fourth birthday, I sat down at the piano, turned to page one and began to teach myself how to play. I practiced for fifteen minutes each morning. It gave me something to look forward to, something to think about, and a sense of accomplishment. These were things I had not experienced in a year and a half. It was my salvation.

A few months later, I felt slightly stronger. I thought, 'If I can play the piano for fifteen minutes each day, why couldn't I spend that time doing something useful?'

I began by unloading the dishwasher. When I experienced no repercussions, I decided to try something else. I did a load of wash on a weekday morning, but found I did not have the strength to lift the wet clothes out of the washer. After that, I did laundry on weekends so that Daniel could transfer the wet clothes into the dryer. When the dryer finished, I was able to fold the clothes and put them away.

Gradually, I became stronger and could stay upright for longer periods of time. When I reached that point, I thought, 'Why should I use up my strength walking the sixty feet round trip to the bedroom and back to the kitchen?' After that, when I got tired, I'd lie down on the floor. This worked very well at home.

Getting my yearly mammogram had become problematic. When going to the appointment, I laid down in the car, but invariably, I had to stay upright for forty-five minutes to an hour in the waiting room. By the time I got to the examining room, I was exhausted. I did manage to stay upright until the pictures were taken. When the technician left the room to have the films read, I knew she would be gone at least fifteen minutes. I decided to lie down on the floor with my head on my purse and rest.

When the technician returned, she exclaimed, "Oh, my goodness!" and rushed toward me.

I sat up and put my hand up to stop her rapid approach. "I'm okay. I'm fine." While getting to my feet, I explained that I had myalgic encephalomyelitis and was simply resting.

After that experience, I brought a small pillow with me and informed the technician when she left the room that I would be laying on the floor when she returned.

With improved technology, the X-ray film plates have been eliminated. Computer imaging now does the job instantly, and I no longer have to take a pillow.

Over the years, and with continuing intermittent daily rest periods, I have regained enough strength to do the laundry, most of the cooking and cleaning the bathroom. Occasionally, I have enough strength to do handwork, bake a treat, shop for one hour or enjoy lunch at a nearby restaurant.

Symptoms

Fatigue and Stress

My two worst enemies are overexertion and stress.

The debilitating fatigue is constant. I am always aware of the level of strength available to me. It's highest when I arise in the morning. With each movement I make and each word that I speak, I can feel my "strength meter" decreasing. When it reaches a certain level, I must lie down and rest. If I push myself too far, I will spend the next day in bed.

I never know when my strength will be completely diminished. Because of that knowledge, every time I leave home and go into the public domain, I am filled with fear. I'm afraid I won't have enough strength to get back home without humiliating myself because I have to lie down in an inappropriate location.

Socializing is another stressor. Putting on a happy face and pretending to be healthy is difficult. The fact that I look healthy as a horse makes it worse.

I do not attend social functions with crowds. The noise and commotion in that setting makes me anxious. Keeping that panic hidden takes an inordinate amount of strength. When I do have to go into a social setting, I look for the exits and mentally figure out how I can "escape" without drawing attention to myself.

One of my biggest fears is that someone will ask, "How does having myalgic encephalomyelitis make you feel?"

I don't want to think about being disabled—let alone talk about it. What makes it worse is that I'm not good at verbally describing the symptoms of the disease.

I usually answer their question with another question.

"Do you know how you feel when you're coming down with a cold—tired, heavy, sluggish, and your brain feels like it is full of mush?"

Their answer is usually a head nod in the affirmative.

I continue, "Well, for me, that's an excellent day because that's as good as it gets."

Their response to that is a blank stare and silence.

Ringing in My Ears

I have had ringing in my ears since March 17, 1975. The more fatigued I become, the louder the ringing. Sometimes it gets so loud, I cannot think of anything else.

Inability to Concentrate

A month before I became disabled, I began having difficulty with concentration and mental retention. At that time, I was working in the personnel office of a U.S. government agency.

The government was introducing a new retirement plan option to the current employees, and the new hires would make a one-time choice of their preferred plan. We received the new rules and regulations with instructions on how the plan would be implemented.

Each morning, for that month, I read the first paragraph of the instructions. Each morning, I set it aside because I could not comprehend what I had read.

I'm certain I still could not decipher that regulation. I am, however, able to read uncomplicated material for fifteen to twenty minutes before my mind begins to wander.

After I had been disabled for several years, I sat down at the kitchen table one morning to write a check. I opened the check book to the next blank check and stared at it. I had no idea how to fill it out. After several minutes I thought, 'If I concentrate on each individual entry, perhaps I can get the job done.'

The first space was the date. I knew that and wrote it on the check. Next came "Pay to the order of." I thought, 'That must be the company we owe money to.' I entered the company's name. Then there was a dollar sign with a short line after it. 'This must be where I enter the numerical amount of money that we owe.' I entered that amount.

At that point, the check began to look familiar. The line below the dollar amount was long and ended with "dollars." I now knew this was the line where I entered the written amount of the money owed. I wrote it on the line. I rarely used the "For" line and left it blank. Signing my name was easy.

The onerous task was finally complete.

Cold Extremities

When I first became disabled, my hands and feet were constantly icy cold. After a few years passed, I had adjusted to the sensation and no longer thought about them.

Sometimes I would go into the kitchen where Daniel was working at the counter without his shirt. When I put my hand on his back, he'd jump and exclaim, "Jesus Christ! Get those icebergs off me!"

One summer, Daniel's brother-in-law, JR, parked a motor home in our driveway. In July, JR's son, Jim, came to visit his folks from Seattle. JR, Jim, Daniel and I went inside the motor home so that Jim could see its interior. It was extremely warm inside the unit. I sat at the table; the guys remained standing. While we were chatting, I reached out and put my hand on Jim's bare forearm trying to get his attention.

He jerked his arm away and said, "Jesus Christ! Are you dead?!"

Over time, there has been improvement in my hands. My feet, however, are always cold.

Burning Sensations

Burning sensations in the calves of my legs became constant. Sometimes it feels as if I am standing too close to an electric heater. Other times it feels like a red hot poker has been inserted between my shin bone and the calf muscle. Occasionally, these sensations radiate up into my thighs and down into my feet. When the intensity becomes extreme, I apply cold clothes to my calves for relief.

Sharp Pains

I sometimes experience sharp, stabbing pains in my skull, collarbones and rib cage. Fortunately, the pain usually passes within twenty-four hours.

Spatial Impairment

Spatial impairment is what I call my crash, bash, smash days. I cannot place a glass in front of a cup. If I do, and want a drink from the cup, I don't go around the glass—I go through it. In addition, I bash things in and out of the sink, microwave oven, dishwasher, refrigerator, and am continually dropping things.

It's fortunate that the majority of the time I drink water because when I wipe up those spillages from the carpet, I call it spot cleaning.

Immunizations

I took flu shots from their inception until the late 1970s. The last one caused a terrible reaction. I was sicker than if I had contracted the flu. I did not get another flu shot for almost two decades.

After I became disabled with myalgic encephalomyelitis, Dr. H became concerned because I continued to refuse the flu shots. Since my immune system was now compromised, he feared I would become far more ill if I became infected with a flu virus.

In the mid-nineties, he showed his usual concern and added that the shots no longer had an egg base. He had always maintained that was why I had reacted to the last shot I had taken.

I finally relented and let him inject me with the flu vaccine. Three days later, I relapsed. I was once again flat on my back in bed.

I was angry. I was depressed. The crying returned.

It took six months to get back to where I had been prior to that shot.

Dr. H never again suggested a flu shot, and I've never allowed *any* injection that would have an effect on my immune system.

CHAPTER 2

SUICIDE ATTEMPT

When I realized I was not going to recover from the myalgic encephalomyelitis in a year, I knew I would be disabled for the remainder of my life.

After taking the sleeping pills Dr. H had prescribed for several years, I began thinking it would be a good idea to have an extra supply on hand in case I decided to put an end to my life.

I skipped a pill now and then and placed it in another bottle. When a thirty-day supply had accumulated, I saved the new prescription pills and took the "old" ones. That way I would always have the most recently purchased pills available if the need for the final solution arose. This routine continued for years.

In early 2006, I began having digestive problems. Every time I ate, I felt deathly sick. When I would begin to feel slightly better, it was time for the next meal. Again, I felt deathly sick. I decided it was time to accumulate additional pills. In five months, I had another thirty.

Dr. H wanted me to have a colonoscopy to try and determine what was causing my digestive tract problems. Just the thought of preparing for the colonoscopy kept me from calling and making an appointment. I kept feeling worse and worse, and in July, I did schedule the procedure for late August.

Shortly after that call, the insomnia became worse. Two weeks later, I had my sleeping pill prescription refilled. I now had a total of ninety tablets available to me.

I had been disabled and a useless drain on society for twenty years, eating made me deathly sick, and now I could not sleep.

The time had come to end my life.

I wrote a short letter explaining my actions and saying goodbye to Daniel and my family.

I don't recall how I decided on the specific day. At bedtime on that evening, I placed the three bottles of pills and a large glass of water on the bedside chest in my bedroom. I wondered if that much water would prove to be problematic.

Placing my pillow vertically against the headboard, I got into bed and leaned back. I poured some pills into my hand. As I looked at them, I wondered, 'Will ninety be enough? Surely, if one pill provides me with a few hours of sleep, ninety will end my life.'

I put the pills into my mouth, but suddenly felt afraid. I began taking slow, deep breaths and thought, 'Do you really want to do this?' The answer was a resounding, 'Yes!'

'For heaven sakes,' I thought, 'Mom did it three times! If she can do it, so can you. Stop being such a coward!'

Taking one last deep breath, I began swallowing the pills. I used small amounts of water—just in case. I didn't want to be awakened because I needed to urinate.

It seemed to take a long time to get the ninety pills swallowed, but the task was finally completed. I put the caps back on the bottles and placed them and the water glass neatly on the chest and shut off the lamp.

I settled myself into bed. Lying on my back, I folded my hands across my chest. I was in the proper casket pose. The thought of that made me smile, because in my mind's eye, I was gripping a large, white calla lily.

Two additional thoughts made my smile broaden. 'First, I would soon be seeing the family and friends who had gone before me, and secondly, I would no longer be sick.'

I laid quietly, breathed slowly, and waited for the end. Peaceful sleep came.

When I opened my eyes, I was looking at Dr. H's face. I gave him a big smile and said "Hello!" and went back to sleep.

I don't recall any other events that occurred while I was in the hospital. I do know that I got hours and hours and hours of much-needed sleep.

After a short stay in the hospital I was taken, by ambulance, to a recently built mental health facility on the hospital's grounds. That's where I spent my legally required seventy-two-hour hold. I had a nice two-bedroom all to myself.

The morning of my first full day, I still felt groggy. I was lying in a standard twin-size bed when a woman came in and sat in a chair beside me. She introduced herself—a psychiatrist. She had a very sad look on her face and spoke quietly.

Giving me a sweet, sympathetic smile, she said, "Tell me one good thing about yourself."

"Just one?" I asked. I brought my hands out from under the covers and, looking at the ceiling, I counted on my fingers as I spoke.

"Let me see now. I'm honest, hardworking, dependable and reasonably intelligent."

I paused, and then continued, "I'm also a kind, gentle, thoughtful, compassionate person."

I stopped. "Guess that's all I can think of right now."

When I glanced at the doctor, I did a double take.

Her mouth was a gaping hole. She closed it and said, "I have *never* had a patient respond like that!"

"That's probably because your other patients are clinically depressed. I'm not. I'm here because I didn't want to feel sick anymore."

She looked baffled, but managed to say, "I see." She left the room without further comment.

I had arrived at the facility in a wheelchair and was advised to use it at all times. When I awoke on the second morning, I felt far less groggy. I looked at the wheelchair and thought, 'I don't think I need to use that.'

With great caution I put my feet on the floor and slowly stood up. 'So far, so good,' I thought. Taking the same precaution, I walked toward the end of the bed keeping my right leg against the mattress. When I reached the end of the bed, I wondered, 'Can I make it from here to the sink? I think I can.'

I took several small steps; I was in the middle of the room. I was very pleased because I was maintaining my balance. I took two longer steps and fell backward like a freshly hewn lodgepole pine. I hit the floor with a thud.

Fortunately, a staff member was passing my door just as I landed. She rushed in, helped me up, and kept me steady until I was seated in the wheelchair. She was very concerned that I might be hurt. I assured her I was not.

For the remainder of my seventy-two-hour hold, I stayed firmly planted in that wheelchair.

The same evening after I had fallen, I was brushing my teeth before retiring for the night. When I looked at my tongue in the mirror, it was covered with a thick brown carpet of "stuff." I could neither brush it nor scrape it off. If it had been green, it would have looked like a rampant chia tongue. It turned out to be oral thrush and was treatable.

When going from place to place inside the facility, I used my hands to change the wheelchair's direction. Once I was headed in a straight line, I propelled myself with my feet.

There was a downhill incline from the west door of the building onto the patio. When someone opened the door for me, I'd make a "run" through it and then raise my feet as I rolled to the patio's edge. Each time I did this, I would exclaim, "Wheeee!" until I came to a stop. The other patients enjoyed my antics.

The majority of the patients were in their twenties and thirties, and each had their own experience to share. All were generous with their advice on what substances *not* to ingest when a suicide attempt was made. Tylenol was on the top of everyone's list. Apparently, when taken in large doses, it causes liver damage.

After the seventy-two-hour hold was completed, I went home. The struggle with myalgic encephalomyelitis, digestive problems and insomnia continued.

In October, I managed to prepare for the colonoscopy. Dr. Roberts also did an endoscopy. It was during that procedure he discovered five peptic ulcers.

Three weeks after taking the medication he had prescribed, I no longer felt deathly sick when I ate. Six months after that, I was back to my "usual" self.

CHAPTER 3

ALLERGIES

I was born with allergies, but they did not present the usual symptoms that a doctor could recognize. For the first sixty-three years of my life, my allergies went undiagnosed.

In the late nineties, I began experiencing difficulties breathing during the summer months. Having been addicted to cigarettes since I was eighteen, I figured the effects of my bad habit were catching up to me.

In the spring of my sixty-third year, Daniel and I moved to an HOA community.

A month later, my skin became hypersensitive to humidity and air movement. I could feel the air's moisture moving up over my feet and onto my calves. At the same time, I felt the dampness settling on my head and shoulders. My clothing felt like it should be removed and wrung out. When the refrigerator motor ran, I could feel the air movement it created.

To ease the annoyance around the house, I cut paper grocery sacks open and placed them on the kitchen chair I used and my end of the couch. I had additional paper cut to cover the entire surface of the couch to allow me to lie down and rest.

At night, I covered the bottom bedsheet with paper. I placed pillows down the sides of the mattress to keep the upper sheet from touching my skin. I *was* able to tolerate the sheet and blanket to just touch my neck to keep out any drafts.

Since I was using so many grocery sacks, Daniel purchased rolls of brown wrapping paper, which made the task quicker and easier.

Around the house, I placed a jumbo dish towel on my head because it was large enough to cover my shoulders, too. I wore my muumuu and thongs (flip-flops to the younger generation) on my feet.

When a situation required that I be fully clothed, I felt as if I would go out of my mind from the irritation.

For decades, I had developed many symptoms that no doctor could diagnose, so I put off making an appointment when this new problem arose.

After being my physician for thirty years, Dr. H became semi-retired. When that occurred, I decided to select a physician closer to home. I chose Dr. Rich whose office was across the street from our house. When we moved to the HOA community, his office was a mile and a half away.

After tolerating the hypersensitive skin symptoms for three months, I called and made an appointment with him. When I described my problems, he thought it might be caused by a hormonal imbalance. A blood test revealed it was not.

Even though I had never shown the usual symptoms of allergy sufferers, he wanted me to see a specialist in that field.

When I made an appointment with the doctor he recommended, I followed his staff member's instructions on what food and medications *not* to be ingested prior to my first visit.

Six weeks later, I was shaking hands with Dr. Jeffries. I told him he had been recommended to me by Dr. Rich and described my symptoms. In his turn, he asked various questions which I assumed were necessary to make a final diagnosis.

His assistant took me to an examining room to prepare me for the test. She was an extremely nice woman with an obvious sense of humor.

I was instructed to remove my blouse and bra. She held a cotton cover-up in front of her so that I could put my arms through the sleeve openings. When I did as instructed, I didn't stop until my arms encircled her and I gave her a hug.

"That's a first!" she said. We both laughed.

I was lying on my stomach atop the examining table when she began writing on my back using a black magic marker. My back was covered with numbers that would coincide with the allergens to be injected.

When the injections were complete, she left the room. After the required time had elapsed, she returned and began making notations on the form attached to a clipboard. Never having had any allergy symptoms, I assumed that everything would be normal.

When Dr. Jeffries entered the room, he reviewed the notations and informed me that I was allergic to cottonwood trees, thistles and a "lesser" dust mite.

I was shocked, but hopeful. Perhaps this time someone could help me.

I was given a thirty-day supply of Nasacort and instructed on its proper usage. I went home and began my daily inhalations. Because I did not have any of the usual allergic symptoms, I had no idea how I would know if the medication was working.

One month later, I had my second appointment with Dr. Jeffries. I told him that I had not noticed any changes and *definitely* had not experienced any improvement.

This time I was given a thirty-day supply of Veramyst. This medication required a somewhat different mechanism to expel the mist, but I was able to accomplish the task. I began using it when I got home.

Two weeks later, I was standing at the kitchen sink. Suddenly, my body felt lighter. The weights I did not know I had been carrying my entire life had been removed. I stood erect.

At the same time, I turned my head and looked out the sliding glass door into the yard. I closed my eyes tightly and opened them again. I could not believe what I was seeing. I never knew the world was so bright and clear! It was as if someone had removed a thick gray veil from before my eyes.

I took a deep breath and said aloud, "Wow!"

This miraculous change lasted but a few seconds. I wondered if I would experience it again. During the next two weeks, it happened twice—each with a brief duration.

At my next appointment, I expounded the miraculous changes to Dr. Jeffries.

He was extremely pleased. "Veramyst is a slow-acting medication. It could take up to five years for you to feel its full potential."

I had walked around for sixty-three years carrying a lead shield and wearing a gray veil in front of my eyes. I could wait a few more years to have the "wow" experience on a full-time basis.

It took a year and a half to have the "wow" feeling the majority of the time. My entire life had changed. Seeing the world so clearly and brightly put a continuous smile on my face. I was so pleased to have enough strength to stand erect that I was walking around like an Army private approaching an officer.

After three years, I occasionally had brief moments with even clearer vision which lasted for a few minutes. Is "wowier" a word?

*****

The second summer Daniel and I lived in the HOA community, three other properties went on the market. Our realtor sold the house directly behind us to one of her clients who was also a personal friend.

During the time prior to the closing dates of those properties, she called and asked Daniel and I if we'd like to tour the houses as two were vacant and the third was now owned by her friend. We agreed to a time and place to meet.

The first house was nice, although the inside of the microwave was, in my opinion, filthy. She said I was the first person she had ever seen open a microwave's door while touring a house.

The second house had had a water leak in the basement. The carpet was pulled up and had various items placed under it to allow for air circulation. Box fans were running in strategic spots. The area was damp and had a musty odor. I tried not to breathe too deeply.

The third house was the one she had sold to her friend. It was a beautifully appointed home, and our new neighbors were happy to show us around.

As we descended the stairs to their basement, I thought I smelled moth balls. Once inside the living area, there was no doubt about it.

The owner took us into a storage room where she kept her off-season clothing and their accessories. Moth balls were strewn over every flat surface. There must have been hundreds of them.

The odor took my breath away; I began having difficulty breathing. I had to get out of the basement and get to fresh air. I ran up the stairs and out their back door.

That afternoon, I was sitting on the couch in the family room when my back began to itch. I went to the bathroom and looked at it in the mirror. It had red splotches. As I checked further, the rash was on the rest of my body, too. By morning, there were several welts a half-inch in diameter. Each had a white spot in its center and looked similar to a very large pimple.

Following my usual practice, I did nothing and hoped that the problem would go away.

When the welts appeared on my face, I could not distinguish them from my usual pimples. In the beginning, I treated all of them like pimples and tried to squeeze out their core to relieve the pain.

When it was a welt, squeezing made it double in size and took twice as long to heal. Once I figured that out, I no longer squeezed anything on my face.

After two months there had been no improvement, so I made an appointment with Dr. Rich. He didn't know what it was. He drew blood and recommended that I wash with the coolest water I could tolerate and gave me a prescription for a steroidal topical ointment. The cool showers helped; the ointment did nothing.

I returned in two weeks for the blood test results. As usual, the blood test revealed nothing.

Next, Dr. Rich took a biopsy of the largest welt which was on my right shin. The results of this test showed that the welt was indicative of vasculitis. This meant nothing to me, and he didn't make any further suggestions.

As long as I showered in cool water, my skin was normal. I continued to have the eruptions on my face and skull.

*****

At the same time the rash began, my sense of smell became hypersensitive.

I had always had a problem with the odor of perfumes containing musk. Now I lost my breath when exposed to most chemical odors, e.g., fertilizers, household cleaning products, paint, scented candles, moth balls and all perfumes. Whenever I went into a store with these products, I wore a painter's mask and avoided the area where these products were displayed.

At home, I began to smell the odor of natural gas in several locations. When I told Daniel, he insisted it was my imagination.

I asked family members, neighbors and several workmen when they were in the house if they could smell natural gas fumes. No one could.

To my nose, the odor kept getting worse. I called the Public Service Company.

When I told Daniel someone was coming to check for gas leaks, he was angry.

When their company employee had given the house a thorough check using his gas detector, he confirmed we had five gas leaks—two large; three small. He red-tagged our meter.

Instead of being pleased, Daniel was livid. He did not want to pay for the repairs to stop the gas leaks.

I'd had years of experience dealing with Daniel when he was angry. My preferred method was avoidance. In this case, however, our health was my major concern.

I knew I had done the right thing because I have always said, "It's better to be safe than to be blown into itty-bitty pieces."

CHAPTER 4

MARRIAGE AND DIVORCE

In order to understand the path of my marriage, I must share an overview of the first nineteen years of my life.

Growing Up

My parents each played a role in the development of my psyche.

My father had some good qualities; Mom had many. She provided countless happy childhood memories; my father, none.

My Mother

Mama was an optimistic, positive, outgoing person with a great sense of humor. She thought we had a happy family. My sister, Luanne, and I knew we did not. To please her, we pretended we did.

Mom avoided all confrontations. While growing up, her behavior instilled in me the fact that my purpose in life was to please and appease everyone, to keep my mouth shut, do as I was told and never make waves or rock the boat.

When someone did something I didn't like, I would smile and say, "That's okay, I don't mind."

The truth was, it wasn't okay and I *did* mind.

After reaching adulthood, Luanne and I agreed that Mama was what we called man crazy. She was neither promiscuous nor adulterous. She simply enjoyed having men pay attention to her. In her world, *the* most important thing in life was having your own man.

When I was in the fourth grade, Mom began exerting pressure on me by asking, "Do you like any of the boys in school? Do any of the boys pay more attention to you than the other girls? Who do you think is the cutest boy in your class?"

I didn't like her questions because they made me feel self-conscious and uncomfortable. I did, however, think that in order to please Mom, I should *try* to attract one of them.

<u>My Father</u>

My father was a negative, pessimistic, crabby man. His one redeeming grace was the fact that he was a conscientious, responsible man who always found work and supported the family.

Criticism was frequent; praise nonexistent. No matter how hard I tried or how well I did, he always found something to criticize. My most memorable example of this occurred while I was in high school.

I brought home a report card with all As; one of them being an A-minus. When I showed it to my father, I expected, for once, he would praise my achievement. He slowly perused the card—front and back—which peaked my anticipation. Finally, he pointed to the A-minus and said, "That needs work."

I was crushed.

My fear of male authority figures began with my father. It wasn't fear of physical abuse. I feared that I would say or do something he didn't like which would cause him to raise his voice. Not knowing when these events would occur, I spent my time around him filled with dread.

Whenever Luanne or I asked my father if we could do something fun, he always responded with an emphatic, "No!" He loved making us beg.

The closest my father ever came to complimenting Mom, Luanne or me was when we prepared an evening meal that he liked.

He would say, "That was damned near fit to eat!"

I don't know about Mom and Luanne, but his back-handed compliment always made me feel insulted.

Because of my father's constant criticism and lack of encouragement, I left home with no self-confidence and low self-esteem.

Courtship

Most of my dating experience consisted of going out with high school boys and one young man who was in his first year of college. My date and I would usually see a movie or go bowling followed by a stop at a drive-in or pizza parlor.

I met Daniel when we were both employed by a company that was a contractor to the federal government.

He was just my type—tall and thin. He had beautiful blue eyes and eyelashes that any woman would envy.

At that time, the boys and men in my circle of acquaintances were clean-cut. Daniel stood out to me because he was also well-dressed. He always wore slacks and often donned a sport coat. He was neither averse to nor looked like he was being strangled when he wore a tie.

Another attribute was the fact that his personality was the exact opposite of my father's. Daniel had a positive attitude and was always smiling. He was cheerful and had an excellent sense of humor—he actually laughed out loud.

I was nineteen; he was twenty-eight.

On our first date, he took me to a well-known mountain restaurant. Even though it was rustic, it was upscale for me.

The only thing I remember about that meal was the salad. When served, it had a large, bright red cherry tomato perched on top. I had seen these tomatoes in the grocery store, but had never eaten one. I didn't know how to approach this vegetable. I thought, 'Should I pop it into my mouth whole, or should I try to cut this sphere in half?'

I decided to eat the other salad ingredients and moved the tomato around the bowl as I kept a close eye on Daniel's bowl. My plan was to observe how he consumed his tomato and then follow suit.

Alas, I must have blinked at the wrong time because the last time I looked, his tomato was gone.

Rather than appearing ignorant by asking the correct way to eat the tomato, I left it intact on the bottom of the otherwise empty bowl.

Daniel and I continued dating and as time passed, we met one another's families and attended their gatherings. We socialized with his family more frequently than mine because of their closer proximity.

After dating for two and a half years, I didn't seem to be any closer to fulfilling Mom's idea of the perfect life—I did not have my own man.

I was twenty-two years old. My cousins and high school friends were all married and had begun their families. I feared I was going to be an old maid.

Four months later, I told Daniel, "Either we get married or we stop seeing one another."

The following day, he went to a jewelry store and purchased a beautiful emerald-cut diamond engagement ring. The wedding took place three months later.

MARRIAGE

Our wedding was a simple service with only our immediate family members and Daniel's lifelong friend, Joe, in attendance. After the ceremony, Daniel and I paid for a luncheon for everyone at our favorite restaurant.

Since we were both scheduled to take a Civil Service Commission's examination the following morning, we had dinner at a nearby mountain restaurant and then spent our first night at a motor lodge west of Denver.

Meet Mr. Real

While Daniel and I were dating, he was a positive, optimistic, cheerful person. He remained that way throughout our wedding day.

When I awoke the first full day of our marriage, everything changed. I sensed a different feeling in the room. I couldn't describe it, but it was definitely there. The change was Daniel. He had become someone I had never met.

I wondered if, when he woke, he was struck with the fact that after being single for more than thirty years, he was now permanently tied to me. Perhaps he regretted his actions and wished the marriage had not taken place.

I didn't ask any questions; I simply went with the flow. We got ready for the day, left the room, and went to the motel's restaurant for breakfast.

When we walked in, Daniel became the man I had dated—smiling and cheerful. I was delighted! He remained pleasant throughout the meal.

The next item on our agenda was the Civil Service Commission's examination being given at a hotel in downtown Denver. We got into the car, drove to the freeway, merged into traffic and headed east.

Again, Daniel became the man I did not know. He began complaining. First, he complained about the amount of traffic.

I countered with, "It would be worse if it was on a weekday morning. Saturday traffic is much lighter."

It was obvious he didn't like me disagreeing with him which would explain why his next complaint was more vehement. He said that the examination should have been given at the Federal Center which was in our vicinity. That way we wouldn't have to drive so far.

I countered with, "Since people will be coming from suburbs all around the city, the Commission probably decided to choose a central location so that no one would have to drive all the way across town."

The look on his face after I had contradicted him twice told me it was time for me to shut up.

He then began to complain about the incompetent drivers. He used foul language to criticize the driver in front of us for his lack of driving skills.

I said nothing.

When we entered the downtown area, we began looking for the cheapest parking lot that wasn't too far from the hotel. Once again, he complained that if the test had been given at the Federal Center, he wouldn't have to pay for parking.

When he made his choice, we drove into a small lot and parked the car next to the attendant's enclosure.

A pleasant young man came out and Daniel told him how long we expected to be gone and paid him the required amount. As the attendant got into the car, I turned and started to walk toward our destination. His feet remained planted as he watched the car being parked.

Daniel had worked as a parking lot attendant when he was in high school. He criticized the young man because he had driven the car too slowly and had left too much space between our car and the one next to it. This action, it seemed, would reduce the total number of cars parked on the lot and, therefore, income would be lost.

My comment to him was, "Considering he didn't hit anything, I think he did an excellent job!"

We walked in silence to the hotel and upon our arrival were directed to a large space that was set up like a class-room. There were steno chairs and Daniel and I selected two that were close to the exit.

When test time came, the double doors to the room were closed. The examiner explained the rules, types of questions in the exam and the time allowed for each sec-tion. He gave suggestions on the best way to complete as many answers as possible to improve our scores.

Daniel was pleasant to people we had encountered until the tests were being distributed. He leaned toward me and criticized the examiner who had given the instructions. I said nothing.

After completing the exam, we returned to the car, drove to the freeway and headed west. His complaints on the way home were identical to the ones he had spewed on the way down. His additional complaints related to the incompetent person who was in charge of giving the test *and* the stupid questions posed on it.

I tried to change the subject to something pleasant but to no avail.

When we arrived on our side of town, we stopped at his mom's house. His youngest sister and her husband were there. Once again, Daniel became the man I had dated.

It didn't take me too much longer to realize that the man I lived with was the real Daniel. I don't know when his other persona developed, but by the time we married, he had perfected it. Everyone thought he *was* the man I had dated.

Over time, I became acutely aware of the transformation signs and what triggered his change.

When we were alone, Daniel's face was sullen, his shoulders drooped, his attitude negative and his tone of voice was that of an angry person.

Whenever someone he knew called, came to the house, or when we were out in public, his other persona emerged. A smile appeared on his face, he stood erect, his attitude became positive, and his tone of voice was that of a cheerful person.

Living with Mr. Real

The first year of my marriage to Daniel was far and away the worst because that's how long it took me to figure out what I could say or do without causing him to yell.

He was a frustrated man. In his opinion, he could run the world better than any of its leaders, and he despised any person with money or power.

Daniel loathed organized religion, especially Christianity, and thought anyone who believed in any god was an idiot. He had a thick file containing articles from newspapers and the internet that debunked the practice of religion which bolstered his own beliefs.

People who liked team sports, hunting or fishing were also high on his idiots' list.

Since every relative and friend we knew qualified for one of his categories, visiting with them was a challenge for me. If one of those subjects came up in conversation, I quickly tried to change it. If I was unsuccessful, I knew what I would face after the guests left.

Because Daniel displayed his cheerful persona while we had guests, he said nothing. Once they left, I had to listen to him call them names and rant about their ignorance.

The Rope

Daniel was a hardworking man and a jack-of-all-trades who had been blessed with an artistic flair.

One thing we both enjoyed was home improvement projects. We agreed that changing the paint color in a room was the easiest and cheapest way to make an improvement. The best part was it could be accomplished in a weekend.

Daniel's family teased us by declaring that every room in our house was smaller because of the multiple layers of paint.

If there was another type of project that could be completed in a few weeks, Daniel was enthusiastic and worked diligently until it was done. Long-term projects, however, were another story.

I think Daniel could only see a project in its entirety which presented to him an overwhelming feat. I, on the other hand, was able to break down a project into small segments. By concentrating on only one portion at a time, it was easier. Once a segment was accomplished, I'd move on to the next and so on. In time, the entire project would be completed.

Over the years, Daniel told me numerous times about a test he had taken at a university when he was in his early twenties. The results showed that he was an intelligent person, but mentally lazy.

I wasn't sure what that meant, but I came to believe it was Daniel's lack of motivation. I learned that the best way to keep him on track was with my own enthusiasm and goal-oriented work ethic, plus giving him constant encouragement and praise.

This methodology was effective, but it was difficult to maintain. I began to feel as if I had tied one end of a rope around Daniel's waist and placed the other end over my right shoulder with both hands gripping its end. In order to keep him moving forward, I had to pull him along.

When I was healthy and able to work side by side with him, I was pulling him across the plains. When I became disabled, the task changed to pulling him up a hill. After three decades, I felt as if I was trying to drag Daniel up one of Colorado's Fourteeners.

Sleeping Arrangements

Daniel insisted that we sleep in a room with the window open. One of his favorite, and oft-repeated, childhood stories was of the morning he awoke with an inch of snow on his covers.

I have always been a cold-blooded person and liked sleeping in a warm room with the window closed.

When our first winter together arrived, I told Daniel that I didn't want to sleep in a cold room because it made my entire body tense and tied my stomach into knots.

His response was, "Married people sleep *together!*"

Being told that for the remainder of my life—or his—I would not be allowed to get a good night's sleep sent a knife into my core. The loving warmth I felt for Daniel had been dealt a devastating blow.

I began to dread going to bed because I knew there would never be any relief from sleeping miserably.

There were a few times in the early years of our marriage when I gathered enough courage to bring up the subject. This always caused Daniel to rant about what *he* wanted and *he* needed and *he* had to have so that *he* could get a good night's sleep. Never once was what I needed taken into consideration.

After thirty years of periodic begging and groveling, he reluctantly agreed that I could sleep in another room. The price I had to pay for this privilege was fondling his penis every night before we went to bed.

I had traded one dread for another.

Guilt Trip Routines

For a short time at the beginning of our marriage, I tried saying no to having intercourse, but when I did, I was faced with something worse.

Daniel would lay one of his guilt trip routines on me.

Phase One was always the ever popular whipped pup routine. Everyone recognizes it—the drooped shoulders and curved spine stance. The head hangs low and the intended target occasionally gets a pitiful glance from the mistreated pup's eyes.

If I didn't succumb to that routine, Daniel moved on to Phase Two.

He would make himself a cocktail, sit on the front porch staring into space as he purportedly went into a deep depression because of my refusal to have intercourse.

I had two choices. I could tolerate hours of Daniel's guilt trip routines, or I could let him do "it" to me which took twenty minutes.

I opted for the latter.

Sexual Relations

From what I had heard, sexual activity would be less after the first year of marriage. I had been misinformed because the more intercourse we had, the more Daniel wanted. We had sex once a day on workdays and twice a day on weekends, holidays and vacations.

When I balked, Daniel told me that *I* was the one with the problem. According to him, any woman would be thrilled having a husband who wanted to have sex with her so often.

I found that hard to believe, but had no proof to the contrary.

I don't know why I didn't ask other married women how often they had intercourse and if they wanted more. Perhaps I was embarrassed, or more likely, I believed there *was* something wrong with me.

I kept telling myself that I had finally fulfilled Mom's idea of the perfect life—I had my own man. Perhaps I should be grateful for that.

When we entered our second year of marriage, I told Daniel that I wanted to reduce the frequency of our intercourse.

His angry response was, "*I* paid for the license!"

Being told that I was bought and paid for sent a second knife into my core. The remainder of the loving feeling I had for Daniel was destroyed.

From that moment on, the marriage, for me, was strictly a matter of keeping my vows and doing my duty.

I dreaded weekdays, and unlike everyone else I knew, I double-dreaded weekends, holidays and vacations.

The days that I worked postponed sex until evening. On weekends, I'd wake between seven and eight in the morning. Knowing what I would have to do when I arose filled me with dread. Rather than getting up, I stayed in bed. When I heard Daniel coming to check on me, I feigned sleep. Finally, at ten o'clock, I'd force myself out of bed and do my duty.

Once again, I was living a life of let's pretend. This time I had to pretend that Daniel and I were happily married. Using the experience I had gained in childhood, it wasn't anything new—I was already good at it. No one, including Daniel, knew what I was feeling on the inside.

Orgasms

Daniel insisted that I orgasm every time we had intercourse because, according to him, it was good for my health.

Accomplishing that feat when you are having sex with someone you want to have sex with is no problem. Having intercourse with someone to avoid his guilt trip routines presented a dilemma.

How was I going to become sexually aroused to produce vaginal fluids *and* accomplish an orgasm?

Fantasizing Begins

I decided the only way to accomplish my goal was to visualize a sexual encounter with a man I found attractive. Since I had never fantasized before, I was headed into uncharted waters.

My first choice was a computer analyst who worked in the same building. He sometimes came into the office for a discussion with my supervisor, and I occasionally saw him in the hallways where we'd exchange pleasantries.

He was a tall, thin man with sandy colored hair. He had kind eyes, was soft-spoken and had a beautiful smile.

When Daniel was doing "it" to me, I began imagining having a sexual encounter with my fantasy man. Because of this scenario I was able to perform my duty and orgasm. This method worked until...

As I was leaving the building at the end of a work day, I saw my fantasy man walking toward me. We both smiled. As our eyes met, my sexual fantasy began playing in my head, and I could feel the blood in my neck rising into my face!

As we neared one another, his expression changed to a quizzical one. I'm sure he could not imagine why I was blushing.

I kept smiling and as we passed, we both said, "Hello." I increased my speed and was relieved to get a breath of fresh air as I quickly exited the building.

I had learned a valuable lesson that afternoon. *Never* fantasize about a person you know personally.

From that day forward, I selected my fantasy men from television and the silver screen to accomplish my mission.

Coworker's Advice

After we'd been married five years, I confided in an older coworker, Shirley. When I told her the frequency of our sexual intercourse, she said, "You don't *have* to do that!"

When I worked up the courage, I told Daniel what she had said.

His response was to yell at me, "How *dare* you tell *anyone* about our personal life!"

After that, whenever Daniel saw her at social gatherings, it was obvious that his hatred toward Shirley made it difficult for him to treat her in a civilized manner.

It would be two decades before I confided in another person about out sex life.

<u>Fantasizing Ends</u>

After several more years had passed, I found it more and more difficult to orgasm. Fantasizing had become an annoyance.

I told Daniel, "I can't force myself to orgasm anymore. We're going to have to do something different."

The solution was simple—lubricant.

Not having to fantasize freed my mind to travel wherever it wanted to go. My thoughts ranged from what I needed to accomplish at the office, my current sewing, knitting or crocheting project, what to prepare for supper or happy childhood memories.

I knew the required touches and moves for Daniel to achieve his orgasm by rote which made him unaware of my mental absence ninety-nine point nine percent of the time.

There was one drawback. I sometimes became so engrossed with my own thoughts that Daniel, in an angry voice, would say, *"What* are you thinking about?!"

Those words brought me back to reality instantly and my response was always, "I don't know. Sorry."

I then returned to the faked movements and touches and thought about something less mentally engrossing.

Hysterectomy

In the fall of my thirty-ninth year, I was scheduled for a hysterectomy. The night before my surgery, I was sitting up in the hospital bed. Daniel was standing at its foot.

For sixteen years, my only legitimate reason for not having intercourse was my monthly period. During those five days, I manually produced Daniel's orgasms. I didn't want to do that either, but it did provide relief from having to submit to intercourse.

The knowledge that after the surgery I would no longer have an excuse for those brief respites, I said to Daniel, "I think I should get five days a month off for good behavior."

He said nothing, but the look on his face was that of a feral animal anticipating pouncing on its prey when the moment was right. I kept expecting to see drool running down the sides of his mouth.

After recovering from the surgery, intercourse became a constant daily torment. There was never any relief.

During the next two and a half years, my physical stamina and strength began to wane. It became more and more difficult to force myself out of bed on workday mornings.

When we worked on projects on the weekends, I had to lie down frequently as I did not have the strength to stay upright.

Carrot of Hope

Whenever I told Dr. H about Daniel's sex drive, he was always awed by his prowess. He used many complimentary adjectives, but stopped shy of saying, *"Wow!"*

Because of Dr. H's opinion on the subject, I never told him the truth about the effect Daniel's sexual appetite had on me.

For years, Dr. H had assured me that when Daniel reached his late forties or early fifties, he would slow down sexually. That assurance was my carrot of hope which kept dangling just out of my reach.

In the spring of my forty-second year, I went to Dr. H for my yearly physical examination. When I once again mentioned Daniel's sex drive, he shook his head and said, "There are some men who never do slow down."

My carrot of hope had been yanked away. On the drive home, I pulled the car to the side of the road and stopped. I felt my insides shattering into hundreds of tiny pieces, and I sobbed.

All hope was gone.

In the months that followed, my internalized mental and emotional distress began to take a toll on my physical health. That fall I was diagnosed with myalgic encephalomyelitis.

Not Your Responsibility

The summer after our twenty-fifth wedding anniversary, my cousin, Sharon, came to the house and joined me for lunch. She was looking at photos from the small gathering we had had with Daniel's family to celebrate the milestone.

She said, "You look so happy! You're so lucky to have one another."

With a sigh, I made this confession, "I'm *so* sick of lying and pretending."

I then told her about our sex life. I ended by saying, "I'm his wife, and it's my duty to make him happy."

Her immediate response was, "You sound *exactly* like your mother! His sex drive is *his* problem, not yours. And it *isn't* your responsibility to fix it."

She was right. I regretted that it had never occurred to me.

Not wanting Sharon's name added to Daniel's hate list with Shirley, I waited a month before saying anything to him.

I approached the subject this way, "Why have I been made responsible for you sex drive problem?"

"I don't know."

We discussed it awhile, and I said, "How about we only have sex when both of us want to have it?"

He agreed; I felt relieved.

Fifteen minutes later, he was "all over me."

I pushed him away. *"That's* not going to work!"

We had another discussion and agreed to have sex three times a week at a specific time on specific days.

That was an improvement over having intercourse nine times a week, but I still hated every second of it.

Bag of Peas

Not long after our negotiated agreement, my repressed anger about our sex life had reached the point that I wanted to hit something. I discovered that smashing a bag of frozen peas on the top of the chest freezer in the garage provided relief. If I needed to give an explanation for my behavior, I could say that I was breaking up the frozen clumps.

One evening, I was especially angry and needed a "pea fix." I went to the garage and followed my usual procedure. Unfortunately, I hit the bag on the freezer harder than usual and it broke. Peas went flying everywhere. I quietly uttered a few curse words and began the cleanup.

The kitchen door opened. With the light behind him, Daniel appeared to be a dark, menacing figure looming in the doorway

Terror struck.

In an accusing tone, he asked, "What have you done?!"

In my usual wimpy, apologetic voice, I replied, "I hit the bag too hard. No problem. I'll clean it up."

He went back inside.

'Whew!' I thought. 'I just dodged that bullet.'

Psychologist

After the pea fiasco, I knew I needed to see someone. I called Dr. H and asked him to recommend a psychologist.

"A psychiatrist could prescribe medication, if you needed it."

"I don't need pills. I need someone I can tell the truth to about how I feel."

He gave me the name of a male doctor.

"No," I said, "I want to see a woman."

"Why?"

"Because," I explained, "my problem is with male authority figures."

He then recommended Dr. Donovan.

On my first visit to her office, I was surprised by its size. It would have made a spacious walk-in closet. She had a very large desk that took up two-thirds of the space. Her chair had to be placed under the desk in order to open and close the door.

In one available corner was a four-drawer metal file cabinet. Tucked in the other corner was a low, modern Danish-style chair abutted by a tiny end table. Atop the table sat a tall lamp and a large box of tissues.

Upon entry, I introduced myself and "fell" into the patient's chair.

She began our session by telling me about the laws that governed her work. I nodded my head in agreement as she conveyed each requirement.

The last law she cited was, "If I think you are suicidal, I have to report it."

Again, I nodded. I then asked, "What if I'm homicidal?"

Now *I* knew what terror looked like. I saw it in her eyes!

I told her I was joking; she was not convinced.

The session continued.

I spewed out the anger and hatred I had repressed about Daniel's sex drive, and told her that I had spent my entire life being controlled by male authority figures who manipulated me into doing things I did not want to do.

Being able to tell someone exactly how I felt was exhilarating!

During our four sessions, I came to realize that it wasn't the fault of the male authority figures manipulating me. It was *my* fault for allowing it to be done. I felt truly enlightened.

I knew what I had to do, but putting it into practice wasn't going to be easy.

I had spent almost five decades of my life saying yes. Just the thought of *actually* saying no to someone made me nauseous.

I can't recall the first person I said no to, but I vividly recall how I felt when I did. I was light-headed, and did not utter a strong, forceful "no," but rather a timid, apprehensive, croaky "no" that I had to force out of my mouth.

Having that word pass my lips was exciting—my heart raced and I felt powerful. This flush of success was fleeting. It was quickly replaced with my ever present guilt because I had not complied with someone's request.

I continued trying to become a more assertive person. Having mustered up the courage to say "no" once gave me the strength to do it again. What I discovered was that the more I said it, the easier it became to say it again and again and again.

In time, I made great strides with everyone except Daniel. I was still too frightened to talk back to him.

Personal Torment

During the years I pretended I enjoyed having sex with Daniel, my emotional responses toward his addiction went from resentment in the beginning, to bitterness, to anger, and finally, hatred. When I reached the hatred phase, cracks began to appear in my armor.

Sometimes Daniel would hold off his orgasm in order to prolong his enjoyment. From my prospective, it was prolonging my torment.

When I realized what he was doing, I would ask in a controlled, angry voice, "Are you holding off?"

When he answered, "Yes," I continued, "You know how much I *hate* doing this, so just *get* it over with."

The day came when I could no longer tolerate him touching me in a sexual way. I told him that while we were having intercourse, the only thing he could do was kiss and hug me—nothing more.

Because he wanted to continue having sex, he complied.

After thirty-five years of marriage, Daniel was no longer able to maintain an erection. I felt tremendous relief knowing that I did not have to submit to unwanted sex and the humiliation and degradation it had caused.

Infusions

Daniel had been plagued with infected acne since he was a teenager.

When he was well into midlife, Dr. H prescribed the antibiotic, tetracycline, to see if it would help. It was miraculous! Daniel's face was pimple-free for the first time in his life. He continued taking that medication.

Years later, he was diagnosed with osteomalasia caused by the prolonged usage of tetracycline. The X-ray of his pelvic bone had the same crackled appearance as my great-great-grandmother's porcelain platter.

Because of his extreme case, the specialist prescribed massive doses of Vitamin D tablets and quarterly Boniva infusions. The infusions were done at the hospital and took approximately five minutes to complete.

When we received the first notification from Medicare that showed the charges for the Boniva procedure, we were flabbergasted. Its cost seemed astronomical.

Of course, after Medicare disallowed most of the charge, paid their share, and the supplemental insurance paid the remainder, we owed nothing.

Daniel did not consider the end result; he ranted about the initial cost. If it had been a one-time occurrence, I could have overlooked it. It was not. He ranted every time a Boniva notification arrived.

Daniel always collected the mail. If he brought it in, laid it down, and walked away, I quickly searched through it to see if we'd received an envelope from Medicare. Sometimes I was able to keep the notifications away from him. Most of the time, however, I was unsuccessful.

It reached the point that each time a Medicare envelope arrived and I was unable to intercept it, my stomach tied up in knots in anticipation of his tirade.

After several years of this behavior I decided to try something. When I was able to intercept one of the notices,

I got the tape recorder and took it to the kitchen. I sat it on the table in front of him. He looked puzzled.

I remained standing and said, "I want you to hear what I have to listen to."

He still looked puzzled. I turned on the recorder and handed him the notification.

He looked at it and when he began to speak, I had to lean close to him because he was whispering.

"That's not so bad. I don't have to pay for it. Just go ahead and file it."

That ended his tirades on *that* subject.

Attitude Adjustment

Not only did the miraculous allergy medication provide me with the strength to stand tall and see clearly, it also put some "starch" into my spine.

When I'd been taking the medicine for sixteen months, Daniel and I passed our forty-second wedding anniversary.

Throughout our married life Daniel had, at times, said mean, hateful things to me. I always kept my hurt feelings and tears hidden from him, but with each incident, my anger had grown. With my newly found strength and "starch," I decided I had had enough.

One morning, we were going to move a chest of drawers from one bedroom to the other. We had removed the drawers and placed the chest on its top so that it would glide easily on the carpet.

As he pulled and I pushed, Daniel gave me instructions on how to maneuver around corners and how to avoid hitting the walls and other pieces of furniture. I followed his instructions to the letter. As we neared the location where the chest was to be placed, he gave his final instructions which I, again, followed to the letter.

He stopped abruptly and yelled, "What are you doing? That's not going to work!"

I looked him straight in the eye and yelled back, "I'm doing *exactly* what you told me to do! If it's wrong, then it's *your* fault, not mine!"

Not only was he shocked that I had yelled back, it was obvious he didn't like it.

After that incident, I continued talking back whenever I was provoked. The fourth time I did it, Daniel was getting ready to run an errand. I was sitting on the edge of the couch cushion in the family room when he yelled, "You need an attitude adjustment!"

One of my character flaws is being sarcastic. I do try to fight it, but at that moment I lost the battle. With a little grin on my face, I seated myself comfortably on the couch and in a quiet, calm voice asked, "Do you mean to say that you don't like my positive, optimistic, do-what-needs-to-be-done, and make-the-best-of-everything attitude?"

He departed without saying.

DIVORCE

The Rope

Shortly after the attitude adjustment incident, I once again, talked back to Daniel. This time he yelled at me, "It's time we got a divorce!"

A divorce had never entered my mind and his statement shocked me. Not wanting him to know that, I said, "Fine with me," and turned and walked away.

I knew he didn't mean it. It was just another ploy to try and put me back in my place.

The remark *had* frightened me, but it also sent my train of thoughts down a different track. I began to wonder what I would do if we did get a divorce.

I started making mental calculations. I would have my small disability check plus the interest payments on my half of the assets. The combination of those monies would be enough to pay the rent on a small apartment. If I chose a place close to a grocery store, I could walk to it. There were also agencies that provided assistance to senior citizens. The more I thought about it, the better it sounded.

A couple of weeks later Daniel, once again, yelled, "It's time we got a divorce!"

This time I was not alarmed. Instead, with a smile on my face, I said, "That's fine with me. Call an attorney."

Two weeks after that, I was walking down the hall to my bedroom. Daniel was right behind me ranting about something. I don't remember if it was something I'd heard many times or something new.

Whatever it was, I literally put my hands above my head and let go of the invisible rope that had bound us together. I thought, 'That's it! No more! I've had it! It's over!'

I felt like a second weight had been lifted from my body.

I spent the next three days building up enough courage to confront him.

On the fourth morning, I went into the family room where Daniel was sitting on the couch. I sat on the fireplace hearth and said in a calm voice, "You're right, Daniel. It is time we got a divorce. There's nothing left. All we do is argue and fight."

Without any emotion, he said, "If that's what you want, it's fine with me."

I called Daniel's niece, who is an attorney, and she recommended a divorce lawyer. I called and made our first appointment.

Happy/Unhappy

Shortly after the divorce proceedings began, Daniel and I were standing at the kitchen sink. He looked at me and said, "You have made me happy every day of our marriage."

"Everyday?!"

"Yes."

"Even since the divorce proceedings began?"

"Yes."

I didn't believe him, but decided to tell him the truth.

"Well," I said, "count your blessings, because you've made me unhappy every day since the first winter we were married."

Dividing Assets

My father was not a good person, and I never thought I'd see the day when I considered him a better man than Daniel. I was wrong.

When my parents separated, my father made certain that Mom got half of their assets and half of their *combined* monthly incomes.

When Daniel and I began discussing our assets, I talked about being fair and dividing things equally.

Daniel kept saying, "You don't *deserve* half the value of the house. You don't *deserve* half the value of the car. You don't *deserve* half the value of the stock. You don't *deserve* half of the money in the bank. So why should I *give* you anything?"

His attitude brought to my mind a scene from the movie, Gone with the Wind. Scarlett and Rhett are in New Orleans on their honeymoon. Rhett says he is going to buy Mammy a red silk petticoat and Scarlet responds, "I won't *give* her anything if she doesn't *deserve* it."

I thought back to the first year of our marriage when Daniel informed me that *he* had paid for the license. I wondered, 'Had he always consider me his property?'

After his tirade, I said, "The divorce laws of the State of Colorado dictate that the assets of a divorcing couple will be divided equally."

"I don't *care* what the law says," he retorted. "*You* don't deserve it!"

Gifts?

One morning, Daniel and I were eating breakfast at the kitchen table. Without any prelude, he said, "I want you to pay me half the original cost of your good jewelry."

I was speechless. I could not believe that he wanted me to pay him half the cost of my Christmas, birthday and anniversary gifts!

Unable to think of anything intelligent to say, I responded with, "You can have it."

"I don't *want* it!"

I said nothing.

"Oh, well," he sighed. "I guess I'll *let* you keep it."

Survivor Benefits

Two months into the divorce proceedings' process, I was sitting in the family room watching television. Daniel came in. He had a look on his face that I had never seen before. He was ecstatic and smiling from ear to ear.

I smiled back.

"Guess what I thought of?" he asked.

"What?"

"I'm going to call Social Security and find out what I have to do to *stop* you from receiving my survivor benefits just like I did with my Civil Service benefits!"

My chin hit my chest. I was dumbfounded. His vindictiveness knew no bounds.

Too Little, Too Late

For the majority of the nineteen years I worked after marrying Daniel, he and I worked at the same locations. When each of us finished our day on the job, Daniel drove us home.

I had no problem going directly home after work or when we had done our grocery shopping. But on the occasional days when we ran an errand or conducted personal business after work, I felt differently.

I wanted to stop at an inexpensive restaurant to eat. A pancake house was a favored location as we both enjoyed a waffle for dinner.

The problem was that Daniel *never* wanted to stop. I think we differed on this issue because of what occurred for each of us when we went home after our business had been concluded.

When Daniel arrived home, he *got* to have intercourse. He then prepared himself a cocktail, sat on the couch, put his feet up and read the paper.

My routine was that I *had* to endure intercourse which was followed by doing a load of wash, packing lunches for the following day and preparing dinner.

Even though I knew what I would have to listen to after we had completed our business, I still asked the question, "Could we stop for dinner before we go home?"

Daniel never failed to give me the same response. After a three-minute tirade of negativity stating all the reasons why he did not want to stop, he always ended with, "But, if you r-e-e-e-ally want to, we can."

Even though he had taken the pleasure out of it, I always said, "Yes." At least I didn't have to prepare dinner, and I *had* postponed intercourse for an hour.

Just before our divorce became final, Daniel took me to Sears to purchase undergarments. On the way home, he said, "Would you like to stop and get something to eat?"

Never having heard those words pass his lips, I was stunned. 'Surely,' I thought, 'I had misunderstood him.'

To clear up my confusion, I asked, "What did you say?"

Again, he asked the question. I immediately accepted his offer.

We stopped at a cafe and enjoyed a sweet roll, coffee and a pleasant conversation.

After decades of never wanting to stop, I didn't know why he had changed his modus operandi. What I did know was that it was too little, too late.

Duty Done

When I married Daniel, I thought I was walking into a new world filled with happiness and contentment. Instead, I stepped inside an imaginary cage surrounded by bars of my own making—honoring vows, doing my duty, and a determination to never quit.

When Daniel yelled at me that he wanted a divorce, *he* became the quitter. I had honored my vows. I had done my duty. With that one sentence, he removed all the bars from my cage.

After forty-two years, nine months, and twenty days, the divorce became final. I was free.

THE

BEGINNING

EPILOGUE

Introduction

My new beginning began in a small city less than twenty miles from the smaller town where I had grown up.

It was here, as teenagers, we went for fun on Saturday night. There was a movie theater with plush carpeting and the aroma of fresh, hot popcorn in its lobby. It was here that I first saw the movie, Gone with the Wind.

The favorite pastime for teenagers in the late 1950s was slowly "dragging" Main Street in their vehicles from the south end of town to the north end, just past the cemetery and back again. The purpose was to attract members of the opposite sex. I was unsuccessful at this pursuit, but it was where Luanne met her future husband, Roy.

I now live on Main Street in a three-story senior citizen apartment building. Teenagers no longer consider dragging this street a form of entertainment.

Thermostats

One evening when Daniel and I were first married, I turned up the heat when I got cold. His response was yelling at me, "Did you turn up the heat?! It's a hundred degrees in here! Are you trying to kill me?!"

After that, I always asked permission before increasing the room temperature.

In my new apartment I now have complete control of the thermostat. I can turn it up or down whenever I want. POWER TRIP!!!

Do You Smell Gas?

My apartment building has laundry rooms on the second and third floors. When I moved in, I used the second floor laundry room a few times. The first time I entered, I thought I smelled natural gas. Two weeks later, the gas odor seemed stronger. Two weeks after that, I was certain there was a natural gas leak.

I told our maintenance man about the suspicious odor. He went with me to check.

After sniffing the air, he said, "Sorry, I don't smell anything."

"Trust me on this," I replied. "I have a supersensitive sense of smell."

He wasn't convinced.

I continued, "It doesn't cost anything to have someone from the utility company to come and check for a leak. Wouldn't it be better to be safe rather than sorry?"

He agreed.

A few days later, I saw him in the hallway. "You were right!" he said. "There *was* a tiny gas leak, and it's been fixed."

I had been vindicated—my nose was still working.

Where Did I Put It?

After settling into my new home, I began doing more cooking and baking. I enjoyed wearing my new, dark blue denim chef's apron that I had purchased at the craft store.

One morning, I donned my apron and worked in the kitchen. When I had completed that task, I went to the dining room table and did some paperwork.

After resting awhile, I decided to do more kitchen work. I went to the closet where my apron hung on a hook. It wasn't there.

I glanced at the kitchen counter—no apron. I looked in the logical places; I looked in the illogical places. I looked under the couch.

I walked back to the kitchen. Standing akimbo, I thought, 'I haven't left the apartment. The apron has *got* to be here.'

At that moment, I looked down and broke into fits of laughter. I was wearing it.

Facial Expression

With my outgoing personality, I usually smile at everyone I encounter and most of the time, add a greeting as well.

I have always thought it a good idea to become acquainted with the people who work in the stores one frequents.

After moving, I did all my shopping at the discount box store in town. While there each week, I not only smiled at every employee, I also greeted each one with a cheerful, "Good morning!" Over time, I was able to call many employees by their first names.

One morning, after I had selected my groceries, I was heading to the ladies' room for my half-time pit stop.

I was walking down one of the wide central aisles when an employee I had never met came walking toward me.

As we neared one another, I smiled and said, "Good morning!"

"Oh," she said. "*You're* the lady with the pretty smile!"

I was taken aback by her remark and uncertain how to respond. So, as we passed, I smiled again and said, "Thank you."

Q-Tips

Each morning, I take what Mama called a "spit bath." I wash my face, ears, underarms and the "lower forty."

Once I have dried myself, I use a Q-Tip to absorb the excess dampness in my ears that the towel cannot reach.

One morning, a couple of hours after I had laved, I went into the bathroom and glanced in the mirror. The Q-Tip was sticking out of my right ear!

*****

When menopause began, I developed vaginitis. The treatment for this condition is to insert a dispenser filled with the prescribed amount of medication into the vagina. The plastic dispenser is designed like a Tampax injector.

Completing the application is not difficult, but cleaning the residue from the inside of the dispenser is problematic.

Running hot water down its inside works, but is time-consuming and wastes water. I could have purchased a cleaning aid, but preferred using something I had on hand.

It occurred to me that I could wipe the excess medication from the inside of the dispenser with a Q-Tip and then finish the task with hot water. This worked well for several weeks, until…

The day when, after cleaning the excess medication from the dispenser, I came to my senses and realized that I was "drying" my ear with the Q-Tip covered with estrogen cream!

The Mounds Bar

I always take a snack covered with a piece of plastic wrap in my purse when I go grocery shopping. Once I have selected my groceries, I stop and eat it. That snack provides the extra energy I need to complete the remainder of my shopping.

Occasionally, when I reach the check-out line, I find that I need additional sustenance. Luckily, there are always treats available while waiting. On one of those days, I purchased a two-piece package of a bite-size Mounds Bar.

When I got to the sandwich shop where I awaited the shoppers' bus, I quickly ate one of the bars. The second piece, which was still in the wrapper, I placed in my purse.

After I arrived home and put the groceries away, I decided to eat the second half of my treat.

I reached into my purse and brought out the candy wrapper. It was empty. I felt around the bottom of my purse, but found nothing.

I sat on the couch and tried to recall what I had done at the store. I thought, 'I know I was very hungry. Did I eat both pieces? I didn't remember doing it, but I *have* begun doing things and being unaware of them, so…'

A month later I was looking for something in my purse. Having difficulty finding it, I began taking things out.

I felt something warm and squishy. I hesitated and then carefully picked it up. It was the Mounds Bar! I hadn't eaten it at the sandwich shop and, more importantly, I hadn't lost my mind.

The chocolate was no longer shiny. The bar was flatter now and had a piece of fluff on it—which I picked off. I sat down on the couch and began taking tiny bites as I savored my found treasure, which was only slightly the worse for wear.

Man in the Street

The second summer I shopped at the box store, they began selling ladies' baseball caps in a variety of colors for $2.50. Every few weeks, I treated myself to one and soon had enough to match most of my outfits.

The following spring, I walked to the bank which is across the street from my apartment. I always looked forward to banking because the tellers kept a large wicker basket on the counter filled with suckers—my favorite being root beer. As I left the bank, I removed the paper from my treat to enjoy on the way home.

On this particular day, I was wearing pink slacks, white top, a floral blazer with pink blossoms, dark-lensed wraparound sunglasses and a shocking pink baseball cap.

Ambling down the sidewalk, thoroughly enjoying the sucker, a man came out of the florist's shop as I was passing.

Removing the sucker from my mouth, I gave him a big smile and said, "Good morning!"

He returned my greeting and headed for his car parked at the curb. Just as he reached the car's front fender, he stopped, turned and walked back toward me.

I stopped.

"May I tell you something?" he asked.

A bit leery, I answered, "Yes."

"You look as cute as a…"

My eyebrows rose in anticipation and I thought, 'Button?'

He had made his decision. "You look as cute as you can be!"

I gave him another smile. "Thank you. You just made my day."

The Sneeze

My allergist suggested that after the inhalation of my respiratory medication, I use a mouthwash to rinse and gargle. He told me if I didn't, I could start sounding like one of the Chip 'N' Dale animated characters.

One morning, I had just filled my mouth with mouthwash and while rinsing, I walked to the living room. When I felt a sneeze coming on, I returned to the kitchen. I wondered if I could keep my mouth closed and release the pressure from the sneeze through my nose—I didn't want to waste the mouthwash.

When the sneeze occurred, I blew the mouthwash and the accumulated saliva all over the wall above the sink.

I had, once again, learned a lesson on what *not* to do!

Pencil Drawings

Sometimes when Mom was doodling, she would draw the profile of a very pretty woman with a turned up nose, long eyelashes and full lips. I tried to develop that skill, but did not inherit any of Mom's talent.

On a Sunday morning in early spring, I was sitting at the table eating breakfast while reading the comic strips. As I read, I thought, 'Do you think you could draw some of these characters?'

I always keep paper printed on one side only on the table to use as scratch paper. I got a sheet and began to draw. I didn't put much pressure on the pencil, and the lines were drawn hesitatingly.

The results weren't great, but better than I had expected. I persisted. The majority of my initial drawings were about 2"×2". Having no talent, I was surprised, and pleased, with the eventual results.

I continued drawing each morning as I ate my bowl of fruit. The drawings became larger, the lines darker, and there was far less hesitation. As I improved, I began using new paper, and eventually, opted for cover stock paper for its texture and density.

Most of my drawings were comic strip characters, but I did try other things—flowers, earrings, birds, shoes and a tree or two.

Eventually, I used some of my drawings to create three collage-style wall hangings and a dozen greeting cards.

After I had been drawing for two and a half years, I found out that I was gluten-intolerant. Realizing I would never again be able to enjoy a piece of hot, buttered San Francisco sourdough toast was devastating.

At the same time, I began having problems with my drawing. In the past, when I began a drawing, I would make one or two false starts before getting the proportions correct. It now took a dozen or more. Because of that frustration and the inability to complete a drawing, I stopped trying.

Since the loss of my drawing ability coincided with giving up gluten, my brain began formulating a plan, and I thought, 'Let's have a little fun.'

My cousin, Loren, knew about the difficulty I was having with my drawing as well as the fact that I had stopped eating foods containing gluten.

The next time I saw him, he and his partner, Don, took me to breakfast. We were seated in a booth that was raised one step above the floor. We perused the menus and placed our orders.

About halfway through the meal, I said to Loren, "I think giving up gluten is the reason I can't draw anymore."

I had expected laughter, but instead, I heard dead silence. I thought, 'Guess it wasn't funny.'

We continued eating and talking about other things. Five minutes later, Loren said, "I don't think that's possible."

"What's that?"

"I don't think it's possible that giving up gluten could interfere with your drawing ability."

I laughed. "Of course not," I said. "It was a joke!"

"Oh," was his only response.

I was intrigued by the fact that he had *actually* considered what I said could be true.

Several months later, I decided to try it one more time. I went to breakfast with my high school girlfriends—Carol, Hope and Jane.

At separate times during our meal, I apprised them of the difficulties I was having with my ability to draw, and that I was no longer able to eat foods with gluten.

After our meal, we returned to my apartment where we sat down in the living room and continued visiting.

When there was a lull in the conversation, I said, "You know, I think giving up gluten is the reason why I can't draw anymore."

As with Loren, there was dead silence. This time I watched their faces as they tried to reconcile what I had